Signs of the Universe
The myth of the uprising

Francisco Rodrigues Júnior

Rodrigues Júnior, Francisco.
Signs of the Universe: The myth of the uprising/ Francisco Rodrigues Júnior / English version. Montes Claros: Editora Unimontes, 2014. 151p.:il.

Bibliography.
IBSN **978-85-7739-529-3**
1. Brazilian literature. (English version) 2. Deconstructionism. 3. Linguistics. 4. Religion. 5. Myth. Rodrigues Júnior, Francisco. II. Title: The myth of the uprising.

1. My people listen to my teaching; tilt your ears to what I have to say.
2. In parables I will open my mouth, I will speak riddles of the past;

3. What we have heard and learned, what our parents have told us.

4. We will not hide them from our children; we will tell the next generation the praiseworthy deeds of the Lord, His power, and the wonders He has done.

5. He made statutes for Jacob, and set the law in Israel, and commanded our forefathers to teach it unto their children,

6. so that the next generation would know it, and the children that were yet to be born, and them, in turn, would tell their own children.

7. Then they will put their trust in God; they will not forget their deeds and obey their commandments.

Psalm 78: 1-7

SUMMARY

PROLOGUE..7

CHAPTER 1

THE LUCIFER PROJECT 15

CHAPTER 2

LUCIFER'S FURY 25

CHAPTER 3

THE CREATION OF THE WORLD..31

CHAPTER 4

THE CREATION OF HUMANS..43

CHAPTER 5

LUCIFER'S PERSUASIVE BRAND 55

CHAPTER 6

THE ARMY OF ANGELS 65

CHAPTER 7

OUTLINE OF A NEW PROJECT IN THE HEAVEN 79

CHAPTER 8

THE MEN OF THE LANDS OF NODE 85

CHAPTER 9

BEELZEBUB AND SATAN IN THE UNIVERSE 93

CHAPTER 10

THE NODE VILLAGE..97

CHAPTER 11
THE THREE CHEATING ARCHANGELS 107
CHAPTER 12
JAVÉ VISITS THE EARTH..117
CHAPTER 13
THE DEATH OF NODE AND AVENA...123
CHAPTER 14
LUCIFER SUBLEVATION 135
CHAPTER 15
THE LUCIFER JUDGMENT 139
CHAPTER 16
THE NEW LUCIFER' UNDERWORLD 149

PROLOGUE

The world, synonymous with what we give to planet Earth or any other celestial bodies resembling it, did not exist. Just as there was no humanity to which we belong. Everything did not exist, because everything we have today was reduced to nothing. The world was just a void and formless, all hollow, vacuum, dumped and dark; a hole or an endless depression.

If one climbed the heights of infinite cavities (which until now are impossible), one would find an immeasurable place for all science, no matter how modern it was. It was an infinite place, incalculable, to the point of finding no form. The color was an opaque mass of air and the only being in that place was the Verb whose power was contained in the expression of thought. The Verb translated his thoughts through written words as an action to do something pleasing to himself according to the gift of his eternal existence. The past tense and the future did not exist to the Verb. He, therefore, being the beginning and the end, was continually extracting from thought innumerable words, giving each of them its entry, making them organized in large or short sentences. He created the sentences and then revised them carefully to establish consistency with the others. After approving the sentences, he fixed them on his great wall. This mural looked like a large notebook with no lines and no leaves, stuck in the still, gentle wind. With each sentence created, the Verb returned to all previous sentences, until the first. Time was unmeasured, it was acronym, and there were trillions of phrases ready on the windswept wall. The Word created his discourse carefully and in every word contained in his discourse was the mark of His existence in that immeasurable place. To exist meant to be, and therefore it meant to remain, to conserve, to become what one was in something eternal. These words were enough for the Verb to feel virtually edified by the action of constructing them, making them eternal. The sentences were, for the Verb, carefully thought prayers, capable of sustaining him throughout his existence, making him very strong. The Verb never felt alone. The Verb was exempt from questioning about creation; about the Creator and His Creator. The Verb did not know, however, that it was an infinite, self-existent being whose necessary cause would be to create everything that could exist in the universe, including humanity.

The Word had created trillions of sentences and yet summarized them in his speech in just one simple and comfortable sentence that could perpetually nourish him: "I am what I am!"

It once happened that the Verb, in creating a new sentence, found it to be different from all that He had created. The sentence was a maxim of a far-reaching judgment, which was in the present subjunctive of the imperative way to express an order, a request, an orientation or advice. The sentence told Him, "Make angels exist!" He, before creating this imperative sentence, had obviously worked in the field of lexicography by pointing out its meaning to each word. For the word "do" would be "create, execute, construct, grant, manufacture"; for the word "to exist" would indicate the "extent of doing" in the sense of "making something happen" and, therefore, implies synonymous words "being" and "staying", both linked to "being", the most intimate. "Being" would be essential to anything inherent in his perpetual talent for conceiving new things. The word "angels" implied to Him to make exist "a being or thing resulting from its creation", able to be, to exist and to be there with Him, in perfect harmony, as long as it lasted. If the sentence said or commanded, "Make angels exist!" He, though he thought he could only think words, construct them, adapt them, and extend them to their respective meanings, making them available in endlessly revised sentences, to make them unchanging them in his speech; this imperative sentence, from His perspective, would be disapproved.

He thought of erasing it, but kept watching and reading it millions of times. The intonation required by the sentence in the pronunciation brought a different sensation to Him, implying for the first time to give existence to something. I thought, "Let angels exist!"

The Verb never felt tired, and for the first time, after tirelessly reading the sentence and pondering the imperative decision expressed in it, found it necessary to try something new to feel for, though he did not deduce what it would be.

If the word "exist" implied the existence of a reality, the Word was there, somewhere, in an indeterminate seat that, though nothing, boiled down to everything. The Verb, therefore, wanting to find out what he felt, and without realizing what it was, made an extraordinary attempt to study the phenomena proper to that indeterminate place. In his efficient portent, he paid attention to one of the magnificent phenomena, so important that he gave himself lightly to him. This phenomenon made him wander inevitably suspended and called it "plowing", simplifying it as "air." The air, after being recognized and baptized by Him, became strong and carried him suspended by infinity, also acquiring the synonym of "wind". The Verb thought it was very good and did not let the wind carry this sentence. He stood before her and read aloud for the first time, "Make angels exist!" In uttering this sentence, the voice of the Verb resounded throughout infinity and everything shook suddenly, like a physical force capable of altering all movements in one place. The color of that indeterminate seat, based on an opaque mass of air, became vast whiteness, and the Verb, though unique, would henceforth be eternally in the company of hundreds of angels. The angels had ectoplasm spectra resembling, as they moved, small flames of fire highlighting that place. Thousands of angels wandered from one corner to another in favor of the friendly and generous wind that made them keep their radiant and charming fires. The Verb found it all very good and immediately joined the angels, who henceforth would become His legion. The thousands of angels formed an army, which would be one of peace, harmony and eternal justice. He, meeting with the angels and giving them his first speech, realized that from that moment on he would no longer strictly use the written word, but also orally. His linguistic procedures, given the outcome of that angelic creation, would be predominantly verbal.

The Verb realized in its core that all its thought could become an existence through things capable of moving or not; It was enough for Him to make use of the statement, to act with assertion and to obtain the proof, through the absolute trust placed in this idea or source of transmission. This He called faith. Moreover, as he could see faith to be absolute, a commitment to faithfulness to the word given, a noble feeling toward angels created through its maxim possessed The Word. This he found very good. The angels of fire, though lacking the gifts of spoken speech, had the wisdom to assist the Verb in creating new words and their proper meanings by arranging them in sentences, which, carefully, under the aegis of the Verb, they would have to avoid using the affirmative imperative mode and making use of the present or infinitive action time only.

The passages approved and fixed on the great wall and protected by the wind were valid for those who read them for all eternity. As for the imperative mode, only the Word would make use of spoken language. This was the first and great mystery of the Word when it came to the ability to do something in a completely satisfactory way: the action of the right to deliberate, act, and command. The Word asserted that power would not be at the level of possession of dominion, influence or force, but as an ability to impose its will on its angels. This continued until the Word once decided to solve practical language problems, causing some angels to speak. For, being adept at silence, he saw that if all the angels of fire spoke, there would be various rumors, that is, the sounds of speech would break the peace and harmony of that blessed place.

The Verb numbed the angels of fire, made them fall asleep, withdrew from their midst and hovered in the wind for a long time. When he felt able to rejoin the angels of fire, having the solution of the practical use of the tongue, to make it available in that place, he detached himself from the wind and went to be in the midst of the numbing fire angels.

While the angels of fire slept, the Verb, using the imperative mode, made a pinnacle appear in that infinitely flat place, and upon it made his dwelling, building a throne, where he would sit and reign there, as long as it lasted. He had observed that the imperative word implied arrogance, and as he would watch over His creation, he had to take some precautions.

If the word "to reign" expressed a form of state or action, being in the infinitive, it would mean, "to exert dominion over the things created by him." Surely, he would to reign over all things. He concluded: "To reign would be would be to have authority!" Then he realized that he should have in his lexicography field a unique word capable of attributing itself to a strong meaning. In addition, thinking of this possibility, he brought to the word "power" the synonym of "right, reason, or motive to dominate, control, and endure all that might come forth thereafter." The word "power" nourished him with strength and made him feel armed with good ideas. This, he found very well!

After the Verb was organized and armed with its new word "power," he rose in the wind and, in a glider flight, soared high and observed and studied absolutely everything he needed to do from the moment reigned all that infinite place from His pinnacle. That was lasting. When he ceased to soar in the wind, he landed upon the pinnacle and brought to its center a great golden throne. He approached the golden throne and watched him closely. It seemed that he would not use that object to settle, but when, without explanation, the wind grew strong, shaping a series of inexplicable things through fine mists, moving them with harmony and beauty - in a ballet in precise positions." He caught Verb's attention and set him on the throne to patience the beautiful spectacle.

The presentation of the wind was enduring and when it ceased it softly howled the following tune: "Holy, Holy, Holy is the Lord, Verb of this place; we proclaim your glory for now and forever, blessed will be all that will create!" As the wind fell silent, returning to its former peremptory, the Word, seated on the golden throne, thought of the word "saint" and, ascribing the meaning of that word to the goodness, virtue, talent, and aptitude of Ever Being, he breathed the word. He let it invade his insides and felt the word "life" spring from within him, as a condition of his existence, his vitality. He then blessed the wind, calling it the Spirit. He referred to the word "spirit" to the breath and said, "If you say that I am Holy, O air of immense grace! You will not only be a breeze or wind, but the Holy Spirit. Through you, I will give my creation the gift to move them."

The Verb would embody the wind in all its creation, and as an inaugural act of that promise, he, looking down from the spire and seeing the still-sleeping angels of fire, thought of incorporating into them something that honored the wind. He therefore made the angels in his own image, but as to their resemblance, he differentiated them by giving them pairs of white wings, shrouded in light and crystalline feathers. To the angels of fire, the Verb would give the wisdom of how they would handle the wind. The angels of fire, though asleep, as they gained the new bodily form became even more interesting. The Verb came to call them wing angels, and yet, before awakening them and placing them on the windproof to test their wings, He patiently decided to build below the pinnacle a wonderful place where He could quietly accommodate its immaculate population.

Since all the space was infinite, the Verb spread its arms, mapped all the space around its pinnacle, and lovingly, wanting to have all the winged angels close to it, gave rise to a large city, closing it with a golden dome. The golden dome received a light reflected across the throne in the center of the spire, spreading everywhere. The Verb was pleased to have created the city and to see its throne radiate immense light, He sat on it and considered, in a timeless manner, what he would do thereafter when the winged angels awoke. One thing was definite, He would no longer be there alone, and perhaps because of this fact, within his creative process, strings of words with their respective meanings emerged to do; to reign, can do; send out; to order and reign. The word of action "reign" gave the idea to the Verb of "kingdom", a place of bliss, where he and the community of angels would remain; he found all this very good!

The Verb, seated on the throne, looked at the numbing winged angels and blew them calmly. The wind, which was the Holy Spirit of the Verb, caused the winged angels to breathe and rise simultaneously to the Verb throne.

The winged angels flew incessantly in chorus to the pinnacle, where the Verb was on his throne. They wrapped themselves around the throne, flapping their wings harmoniously and expressively. The Verb, feeling the coolness of the breeze through the wings of his angels, and he, in his eternal state of holiness, found it all very good and consecrated them, allowing them to exist forever.

The winged angels exalted the Verb, standing in their respective places. They flapped their pairs of wings without ceasing. In the meantime, the Verb evaluated them by assigning them several timeless tasks. Among these tasks was their role as intermediaries for all of His creation henceforth. He observed that all angels, though created to the same standard in their characteristics and forms, each had their own way of performing each task. In this way, He resolved to observe them individually, giving as a prize an intensity of light to those who would do everything according to His will.

Angels would gain light intensity and become spiritual independents. The first angel to achieve this spiritual independence, the Word would choose him as the leader of all angels. The Verb made a perennial remark that only ended when an intensely enlightened angel caught his eye. The Verb called this Angel glorious, naming it "Lucem Ferre", which means "bearer of light."

Lucifer was the first angel named in the kingdom of the Verb. He became the leader who obtained the authority and charisma to command the heavenly angels. The Verb invited Lucifer to sit on the throne on his right, granting him the divine gift of leading from there all angels. And this angel, image of the Verb, of triumphant light, acted as a leader, lending the Verb all his services, in order to gain the full confidence of all the projects to be carried out in that kingdom which he called "Urbs Verbi" (the city of the verb). He told the angels "everything there deserved respect, because it was a divine and sacred city."

Lucifer glorified the Verb by calling it "Yahweh," which, according to him, would imply the "Lord, infinite, self-existent being." The name Yahweh, according to Lucifer, would designate "the supreme and perfect Being, Creator of all things that existed in that kingdom." The Verb found it very good and accepted the name "Yahweh!" However, he added again, "I am what I am!"

However, Lucifer said he would call the Verb Yahweh and yet greeted him with the expression "Glory to the Lord, Yahweh my God!"

The other angels under Lucifer also called the verb "Yahweh." To Lucifer, the Word was "Yahweh," the angels were simply angels, and he, the leader of all; the great angel, the right arm of the Great Creator of that kingdom where there was peace and everyone worked on creating words, forming sentences, reflecting on them, publishing them on the windblown panels and other projects that arose at will of God Yahweh. All of that thought everything was fine.

CHAPTER 1

THE LUCIFER PROJECT

Lucifer, seated at Yahweh's right, increased his prestige among the angels. He discussed with Yahweh about new projects; designed and executed with angels. Lucifer had some ideas approved by the magnificent Yahweh; Among Lucifer's projects was one that would divide the kingdom into three spheres. In the first sphere, there would be angels who would glorify and behold the Lord; in the second, angels who would gain prestige and authority from the Lord to watch over him on his throne; and in the third sphere, the angels who would be the messengers and those who would obey Yahweh's orders. According to him, each category of angel should have its own sphere, because the Lord would rule them all with his eternal steadfastness and wisdom.

Although Yahweh listened attentively to Lucifer's plans, He found it unfathomable, for to him the word divide would imply "disunity, disengagement," whose procedure might lead to discord. Lucifer tried to convince Yahweh of his project, telling Him "that the whole city would remain one, and that it would be called 'Heaven', implying the state of fullness of the angels with Yahweh, or the House of the Divine Yahweh and His eternal Angels. "

Lucifer said the city would have to be divided into three spheres would have a strong reason to compensate all angels for their efforts. In this way he advised Yahweh to divide the angels into hierarchies, and to each of these hierarchies, an angel would become leader, just like him. To the new leaders chosen in charge of each of the three spheres, Yahweh would give the full condition of administering each sphere, according to their custody. However, Yahweh cautiously argued to Lucifer that this whole city was for everyone and that was all that was good.

Lucifer, more and more, remained obstinate in the idea of dividing the kingdom into spheres. He sometimes looked at Yahweh at the risk of overwhelming himself with a ridiculous presumption, a fact stemming from his overly positive ideas about himself. He wished that each sphere of the so-called "Heaven" had a steward, and he stubbornly thought that, sitting at the right hand of Yahweh, he would also have the legitimacy to govern the three spheres with all his will.

The Lord, seated on the throne, remained silent, just watching Lucifer and his entertainment with the angels. Lucifer felt superior to the angels and made them cheer him up as if they were their Lord. Yahweh clearly saw that this kind of abnormal procedure by Lucifer was not part of his plans for creation.

Yahweh, as he intended to keep everyone there as his perpetual creation, would never interfere with the angels' attitudes, and especially those of Lucifer, "the bearer of light," whom he made seraphim, implying that he was the first position. In the heavenly hierarchy of angels, which would be closest to Him, with the function of leading all angels, garnered because of their full grace? In that city, which Lucifer wanted to call it "Heaven," there was only good and full harmony, fitting synonyms, whose actions served the same purposes as others.

Once, Lucifer, breaking Yahweh's silence, inquired of him about his plan for the division of the kingdom into spheres. He, though anguished, was tenacious enough to convince Yahweh that his plan would be interesting and that this city, or "Heaven," would take on new forms from multiple ideas stemming from his idealizations.

Yahweh, after hearing all of Lucifer's arguments, was impressed, as he quickly drew a location plan through a graphical representation of how he projected "Heaven" by dividing it into three spheres.

According to Lucifer, "Heaven" would be the limitless whole, and Yahweh, Supreme and perfect Being, Creator of all things would exercise dominion over everything and everyone, seated at His throne, seated in the center of the pinnacle.

The three spheres, according to Lucifer's project, would happen so that Yahweh could count on the help of all angels to manage all infinity, since the dome, defining the "Urbs Verbi", would cease to exist.

"Heaven" as an infinite place, Lucifer would integrate angelic beings into a vast hierarchy composed of at least three groups to occupy the three spiritual spheres: angels, cherubim and seraphim. According to him, angels would be the messengers and executors of Yahweh's orders; cherubim would be angels full of wisdom and knowledge, and seraphim would be angels responsible for glorifying the majesty and greatness of the Lord.

Lucifer received Yahweh's approval and carried out his project, discarding the City of the Verb (Urbs Verbi). He built around the spire the three infinite levels. The upper, where would be the seraph (which would be only him); the middle level, where would be the cherubim, and the lower level, where would be the messenger angels and executors of the Lord's orders.

Lucifer suggested to the Lord that he chooses angels to become leader of the two levels, the middle and the lower. The Lord did this, but as he saw and did everything justly, he eventually directed the new chief angels to the higher level, who would enjoy the same prestige as Lucifer.

When Lucifer saw the new leader angels, newly chosen by Yahweh, on his upper landing, he was surprised and quickly went to the center of the pinnacle for Yahweh to explain to him why the leaders would occupy the landing, which belonged to him. The Lord explained to Lucifer that he would choose other seraphim, and they would be on their threshold as the great leaders of "Heaven," just as he would.

Lucifer disapproved of Yahweh's new project on hierarchy, wanted to know which hierarchy he would henceforth belong to among the angels, and especially among the recent leaders, that

Yahweh would also make them seraphim. Yahweh explained it, saying, "Like all leading angels, you will continue to be a seraphim as well; but because of your autarchy, because you have been bestowed with authority and charisma, to command all the angels, you will no longer sit at the right hand of my throne... "

Frightened, Lucifer suddenly asked, "Will Lord Yahweh drive me from the right hand of his throne?"

The Lord continued the speech: "I will not take you off my throne as a punishment, Lucifer. In view of your new project, I prefer to position you inside a chariot of fire that will travel across the sky, constantly leading you to visit the three levels. That way you will be a great leader of the angels of heaven."

The idea of Yahweh comforted Lucifer because becoming a great leader meant that he had authority over all the angels of the new heaven.

Lucifer approved the idea. The Lord prepared a perfect chariot of fire so that Lucifer could visit the whole kingdom. After the chariot was fit for Lucifer's tasks, Yahweh blessed him by driving him according to his competence.

The cherubim, as they saw the splendid and triumphant chariot of fire, admired it, and as a gift to Lucifer's new ways of driving to heaven, they placed an interesting phrase in the carriage: "Praise the Lord for all eternity!"

Lucifer, inside the chariot of fire, accepted the mission with honor, helping all the angels and their leaders in their respective spheres.

Yahweh seeing, perennially, the heavenly angels performs severely in their due tasks, befitting the hierarchies placed at the three levels; he thought it was very good.

Over the centuries, Lucifer gradually became dissatisfied with his task. He felt trapped in the chariot of fire and, disapproving of his project of hierarchies, intended to return to the right side of the throne of Yahweh. That wish would be for him to formulate another project, which could make it conveniently important.

Lucifer's dissatisfaction was because Yahweh gave all the leaders or seraphim the same bodily brilliance and the same commanding abilities, depending on the tasks assigned to their respective levels. Lucifer did not think any of this was good, and he plunged into a disquieting silence, making Yahweh realize that something strange again surrounded him. Yahweh sometimes left the throne and visited the three levels to observe the fulfillment of the tasks of all angels, and exclusively those of Lucifer.

Once Yahweh seeing Lucifer dissatisfied, duly questioned him to know what ailed him.

Lucifer surprisingly asked Yahweh to deliver him from the chariot of fire, to remove him from that post, or to make him no longer exist. He also asked Yahweh to appoint another seraphim angel to become the leader of all the angels in heaven. He no longer aspired to the office imposed upon him.

Yahweh denoted that every request of Lucifer boiled down to the word "destroy" and that word implied for Him a deleterious effect, reducing itself to nothing. He would never destroy what He had created. Everything there was the result of His potency, created by Him, being His and he. Therefore, Yahweh said to Lucifer: "You are the gauge of the measure, full of wisdom and perfect in beauty, I will never destroy it. I will choose another angel to lead you all in your present position and you will sit down again, not to the right, but to the left of my throne. "

Yahweh chose among the seraphim angels another leader to lead the chariot of fire, performing the same function of Lucifer. To the new chosen leader, He named Af, also meaning "angel of light."

Yahweh invited Lucifer to the center of the pinnacle and there anointed him with His blessing, making him to the left of his throne's throne.

Although dissatisfied, Lucifer sat on the small throne on the left of Yahweh and spent a few centuries there studying, writing and trying to insert new designs into Heaven.

All of Lucifer's projects, when studied and analyzed by

Yahweh, failed. This embarrassed Lucifer. Yahweh made him realize that everything was under orders, within the criteria set by him. He argued: "His projection of the three infinite heights, Lucifer, resulted in a perfect goal. Heaven, which you planned, is complete. "

Lucifer, instead of being happy, to hear the positive value attributed to his project by Yahweh, became uncompromising due to the indulgence of his desire for self-exaltation. He was not content to sit on Yahweh's left, nor did he arouse his intention to occupy the right side of the throne. He doubly desired to obsessively occupy the throne of Yahweh and become omnipotent. If he did that, he would make the general plans of his works idealized in his stealth projects.

Yahweh, in all his mystery, able to make Lucifer think that He acted like an ignorant; knowing his dubious intentions, with his omniscience designed a way to place angel on the right side of the throne. This project, Yahweh called the "balance," which would aim at balancing common sense and balance. He, however, if seated in the midst of two angels, would serve very well as a transducer.

Yahweh visited the three spheres and observed all the angels, and drawing upon his assiduous criteria concerning humility, He chose one of the messenger angels of the third sphere to sit on his right. To this chosen angel Yahweh named him Immanuel, saying, "Yahweh is in the soul of the angels, who are mature in being pure and humble."

In addition, there was a great feast in heaven, as the simple angel, chosen by Yahweh, became the seraph Immanuel, who sat at the right hand of the Creator's throne.

Lucifer, though he did not seem pleased with Yahweh's project, kept with himself the cunning jealousy of having another angel as his companion and, in addition, sworn beside the right throne to which he formerly belonged. He thought and feared Yahweh to love Immanuel more than him.

When Immanuel took possession at the right hand of Yahweh, before sitting upon the little throne, he humbly said, "Yahweh, the supreme and perfect being, Creator of all things. Because I have received this abundant gift, behold, I will forever call him God. ”

The name "God," according to Immanuel meant to mean the "Supreme and perfect Being, infinite and existing by Himself, Creator and Father of all things."

In addition, the Verb, known as Yahweh, would give Emmanuel a seat to the right of his throne.

Yahweh, noting that the nickname "God," was a hierarchy or order of varying degrees of power and responsibility, allowed Emmanuel and all the angels of heaven to call him Yahweh.

Immanuel humbly bowed before the Lord, who had made him an angel different from others. He became the most beautiful angel, perfect and endowed with intelligence and self-lights, among all angels, seraphim and cherubim.

Yahweh, eternally recognized as the Lord of heaven, upon seeing the light shining on Emmanuel's countenance, gently said, “You will be my eternal son, who will sit on my right side and share my creation fully with me. You will be like me, and I promise honor before all the angels, to tell you and guarantee my eternal blessing. Wherever you are present, wherever you are present, I will consider your presence equal to mine; therefore your word will have value as much as mine will. Whatever you do, nothing will be for yourself, but for my will contained in you.”

When Yahweh finished giving his speech, the whole heaven trembled, and as it stopped trembling, a bright light appeared in a golden circle surrounding Emanuel's head, making him the image and likeness of Yahweh. Emanuel gained a new feature: a broad and high forehead, noble and majestic, endowed with sublimity and without wings.

Yahweh, convinced of his approval, before the new feature given to Immanuel, said cheerfully, "This is and will be my beloved son forever."

All heaven again trembled and all the angels fell to their knees and worshiped the Father, Yahweh, and the Son, Immanuel, whose image resembled that of the Creator.

Lucifer did not kneel, as the angels of heaven had done. He, sitting on the little throne on the left side of the Creator, merely sought to attain it all. He found it odd that the angel Immanuel, made official to the seraphim post, lost his wings and became different from all the heavenly angels. He soon demanded explanations from Yahweh about the difference in the physiological phenomenon inherited from Immanuel and, especially, the fact that he had no wings. His questioning to Yahweh seemed wanton. The high question ended with a provocative subpoena: ... "Wouldn't Emanuel be harmed because he had no wings and could not fly"?

Yahweh explained to Lucifer that Immanuel did not need the power of wings to fly, because he could translate spiritually everywhere in Heaven, just as He, the Father of all creation.

Lucifer felt inferior to the wonders granted by Yahweh to Immanuel. Among the wonders, the most intolerable would be that of translation, which meant transporting, moving from one place to another and without wings...

After Immanuel seized the right side of the throne of Yahweh, all the angels rose to their feet and flocked to their proper heights.

Lucifer, possessed by envy due to the loss alongside the right throne and the granting of the spiritual transfer obtained from Yahweh to Immanuel, he urged to fly sinuously after the flock of angels, as if trying to reach them.

One of the messenger angels, coming from the third landing, when he saw Lucifer flying sinuously, thought he needed help and dropped the pack, flying toward him. Lucifer, upon seeing the messenger angel coming toward him, purposely barred him. The two collided hard and fell. The messenger angel burned half of his right wing. Lucifer, instead of helping him, flew quickly and retreated to the pinnacle. The messenger angel, though with his defective right wing, managed to fly slowly until he reached his abode.

When Lucifer came to the pinnacle, Yahweh invited him to the seat on the left side of the throne, because Immanuel, an outcast angel, sat on the right side. Lucifer, though dissatisfied, took his position on the throne, deeply resenting Yahweh's invitation as an offense received.

The wind suspended Yahweh's throne, having on the right and left two lower thrones. The two thrones was a balance that measured the weight of the consciousness of the two seraphim.

If there were an imbalance, Yahweh would be able to take proper precautions. In addition, that did not take long to happen, because, as time went on, the balance began to oscillate, with Lucifer's side acquiring nothing-sober attitudes. As the balance unbalanced, Yahweh felt uncomfortable on his throne and the assessment of this discomfort made him deeply sad. He, however, endured; waiting in Lucifer for the faculty of him to realize the meaning of that scale; but Lucifer did not seem to understand the general idea of this divine project.

While Emanuel argued with Yahweh about new plans to be executed in heaven, Lucifer was not sure why, closing his eyes and plotting some sort of plot against Yahweh. He seemed to have motives that are more effective because he had lost the right throne to the angel Immanuel. From this machination of Lucifer came new words in antonym of all that was good in that kingdom; because those words of opposite meanings were retained in Lucifer's mind.

When Lucifer opened his eyes, a strange light in the form of fire sprang from his mouth, instead of beautiful words, strange words came out that Yahweh and the angels of heaven did not know.

Although Lucifer knew that he was an angel created by Yahweh and that his creature could never become the creator, he let the feeling of ambition and envy overwhelm him. He did not want to be a mere creature, but to become the creator, to have power. However, that was impossible, because absolute power belonged only to the Lord creator of everything and everyone. Over the centuries, Lucifer became increasingly blind and proud, and, as he let personal exaltation arouse in him, it was enough for him to find a formula to become independent. He dreamed and did not refute himself the desire to enjoy full freedom and autonomy from

Yahweh.

Yahweh spectacularly inferred dependence; each created thing became the extension of another, a kind of continuity guided by established rules and standards: everything connected at all! This was consistent with the responsibilities assigned to every creature of heaven. The fact that something exists is a dependence on another existence, and so on. Nor was the Creator himself independent, for he sought not to satisfy his needs, but those of his immaculate angels and all those whom He would create.

However, Lucifer, unfortunately, did not see the real purpose of Yahweh, who, though he made him a perfect creature, capable of making him useful in the execution of his great works to come joked the Creator, reasoning him in his morbid spirit. He was willing to serve the Creator in a way contrary to His statutes.

Lucifer had become a mysterious soliloquist, and in his mind populated idea around the word independent. He thought, "I am a creature, and I want therefore my independence."

The prefix "in" used for the word dependence implied a negation, a deprivation that corresponded to the "no", a word that did not exist in the vocabularies of heaven, nor in all of Yahweh's creation. It only came to inhabit Lucifer's mind. The adverb of negation "no" would indicate to Lucifer signs of refusal to everything that Yahweh created and / or could create thereafter. This was very dangerous, because that simple word could radically modify many actions. Something seemed to make him certain that Yahweh created everything in a subjective way, just for his sake, a kind of slavery. By observing the most objective reality, he wanted to be able to perform other actions that could overcome any obstacles. In addition, he became more mysterious, plunging into sober mental solitude.

Even sitting to the left of Yahweh God and with Emanuel, Lucifer seemed inert, unable to discuss any project. Yahweh was full of projects, and only Emanuel seemed interested in hearing and discussing them.

CHAPTER 2

LUCIFER'S FURY

Yahweh looked and thought of all the vastness of space and division that had allowed Lucifer to make the appropriate changes. The "Verbs Urbs" boiled down to just three infinite levels, and in each sphere inhabited a hierarchy of angels. Yahweh realized that several angels were serving Lucifer in some of his ambitious projects that would not be good for heaven.

Yahweh concerned about the imbalance of the balance, because of Lucifer's ignoble manners, thought of modifying the entire space of heaven again. However, if he did so, Lucifer would become more obstinate due to his ideas and would surely rebel against him and the angels of heaven.

Yahweh presented some of his projects to Emanuel, saying that he would do one of those projects called the Universe below the sky. This project would be kept secret, only to be revealed after its execution and approval.

Yahweh, having to leave Heaven because of the fulfillment of the new project, decided to hold an assembly among the leading angels.

The messenger angels blew the trumpets and the sound spread through the sky, serving to announce the assembly that would take place between the Lord and the leading angels.

After the trumpet sound vibrated, the leading angels left their posts in the upper sphere and went to meet Yahweh on his throne.

All infinity fell into darkness causing all the angels of the three spheres to fall asleep. Everything was silent and there were only lights around the Lord's throne where the assembly would take place.

At the assembly, the Lord revealed to the chief angels that he would leave the pinnacle to undertake a project in another dimension.

Yahweh would not keep the angels asleep in the deep silence of darkness while would realize out his project, so he proposed in that assembly that the leading angels choose one among them to occupy an important mission in their pinnacle. Yahweh said, "I will have to leave the throne to do a great work. Choose one from among you to watch over my throne. As long as I am absent, the throne will not be empty, for I will make my light dwell in it, whose radiant energy will illuminate the whole of heaven. Immanuel and Lucifer will not remain on their thrones to the right and left of mine throne, during my absence. The angel chosen by you in this assembly will be alone in the pinnacle where my throne is. He will serve me as a soldier and will watch over the light upon my throne, the brightness of which will extend throughout the sky."

Lucifer, uneasy in his thoughts, noting that Yahweh had just uttered his wish, did he not hesitate to ask the Creator, "Will the angel to be chosen as leader to watch over his light have power over others?"

Yahweh was waiting for this question posed by Lucifer, because of all the circumstances to which he was moving obscurely to the left side of his throne. Then Yahweh answered him, "All heavenly angels have power when they are competent in their duties."

Lucifer closed his eyes, plunged into the darkness of his consciousness and smiled as he declared to himself: "If this asserted by the almighty makes sense, then I learned what I needed. My tool is in my competence, so I have the authority to perform certain acts". He opened his eyes with all their colors, shapes and movements to seduce everyone to yearn for their confidence and to choose him in the sentry of divine light.

Lucifer, unlike everyone, was aiming for the position of great leader. Yahweh clearly saw Lucifer's aspiration, but therefore nothing would interfere with the choice to be made through the leading angels present at the assembly.

Yahweh brought forth a large framed panel before his throne, connecting the spiritual minds of the leading angels to him, so that the choice of the guardian of the light of his throne might take place.

Yahweh's proposal would be to induce the chief angels to sleep, and each, without the interference of him or any other angel would make the choice of the future guardian of light after awakening from their respective sleeps. At the end of the process, Yahweh would show them the result of their respective choices projected on a huge panel.

The leading angels fell asleep, and then each woke up and registered their vow, silently, looking at a light in the center of the panel. This process was slow, and in the end Yahweh prepared the leading angels to give them the outcome of their respective choices.

To the surprise of all the leading angels and Yahweh himself, on the screen of the large framed panel did not appear in the image of Emanuel or Lucifer. In it appeared the image of an angel with a small and defective right wing, whose imperfection would be for Lucifer himself to explain.

After the image of the angel chosen as the guardian of light appeared on the screen, Yahweh awakened all the angels of the three spheres and ordered the messenger angels to blow the trumpets, inviting all the angels of heaven to go to the pinnacle.

Arriving at the pinnacle, all the heavenly angels stared at the panel in astonishment. The angel with flawed wings, seeing his image projected on the large screen, did not believe that such an important mission would be up to him. He did not know whether he would be fit for this important task

When Lucifer faced with the result and seeing on the screen the image of the chosen angel, the one he had injured, was enraged. He spread his enormous wings and withdrew from the throne to the left of Yahweh's, flying out of heaven. He went into hiding in a vacuum, flying over the void. As he flew, he thought emerging: "As a vacuum is nothingness, a void without any aspect, dimension or form, Yahweh or angels of heaven, they will never find me in it."

As Lucifer wandered into nowhere, even bothered by the strong compressed pressure due to the lack of wind, he seemed to want to explode his possessiveness of anger due to the newly chosen spire made through the panel invented by the Creator.

At the pinnacle, Yahweh, as if waiting for Lucifer's sudden reaction, even as he suddenly saw the escape, continued the consummation of the assembly.

Yahweh blessed the chosen archangel and named him Uriel, meaning "Fire or Light of the Lord."

After receiving the blessing of Yahweh to assume the position of guardian of the light of the divine throne, Uriel received the appearance and spirit of a superior angel with immense brilliance.

All major angels praised the Lord and thanked Him for the new role given to the humble angel who not only looked after the herald angels in their sphere, but also of others, never complaining of disability of his right.

The Lord made the huge Uriel wings with golden rays to raise the light of the great throne to which he would remain. After teaching standards to the angel Uriel in particular, he made the light shine on his throne, holding the light rays it across the sky. Uriel took possession of his guardian post; Angels blew the trumpets giving the return message. All the angels in heaven returned to their respective hierarchies.

When Yahweh saw Lucifer's throne empty, he felt a deep sadness. He considered looking for him, but felt that he should not do so, as every attempt to uncover his feelings always made him worse. It was then that Yahweh thought of the word "arbitrariness," noting that its meaning would give "procedures contrary to rules or laws." Yahweh, however, would let Lucifer prove his own judgment, have the ability to discern his wills, and make up his mind. He thought, "Lucifer would be entitled to his free will!"

To the filial angel Immanuel, Yahweh made him invisible, giving him the ability to move into infinity, helping everyone without being seen or recognized. So while he was absent from his throne, Yahweh wanted to protect him from the possible contradictory virtues of Lucifer.

From that moment on, Emanuel would live a new experience enriching his spirit. He said, "Everything the Lord does to us is good!"

CHAPTER 3

THE CREATION OF THE WORLD

Yahweh departed from heaven, leaving the light of the throne under the protection of the angel Uriel. He headed for the vacuum. His proposal would be to disengage for a time from heaven and travel for the realization of a project, whose purpose would be to make the vacuum something comprehensive, giving shape and conditions to connect it to infinity. Heaven's connection between the new to be instituted in a vacuum would seem to be a deceptively link or bridge based on the entity of reason, whose mysteries belonged only to him and no one else. In this way, his creation would become finished and perfect.

The dark, shapeless, weakened vacuum drew Yahweh's attention to a spontaneously flowing method that could help him begin his creative project. He then, looking for a suitable solution, thought of something that could fill the vacuum and give it a new look. He gave the wind order to inhabit the vacuum and both, combining their energies, became stronger, prone to a correct procedure to assist him in the conceptions of his later creations.

The wind inhabited the immense emptiness and became overpowered, but remained pleasantly mild. He, by releasing his stormy energy, made the vacuum an immense blue, and Yahweh found it very good.

Yahweh traveled among the immense blue, allowing him to be touched by the wind and to the unlimited expanse of vacuum, he called it space. He became convinced that space would be the distance that separated the void from heaven, and in that void He would fill it with new things to create and bring forth what would be called the firmament. In addition, He traveled through space with all the pleasant feeling, celebrating the milestone of that creation.

As Yahweh departed from his throne at the pinnacle enduring in the sky, Lucifer, astonished by the vacuum, thought of ways to discover power, with the petty motive of becoming like him. He assumed in his psyche the uncontrollable desire to aspire to the power of its Creator to sit on the throne and to rein heaven according to his wills. For this, he thought, in the malice of his intimate desires: "I must make an insurrection against Yahweh and for me to do so, I must devise good plans."

Lucifer quickly returned to heaven and went straight to the pinnacle, where the angel Uriel watched the divine light from the throne of Yahweh. He tried to approach the throne, but failed; the rays of his light collided with the rays of the light of the throne and made him suffer a terrible shock to the point of blinding his eyes and causing great pain in his body.

Lucifer, previously, did not know what pain was and for the first time experienced it. Blind and with a sore body, he, scared, flew aimlessly, trying to take refuge from Heaven. With many difficulties, wobbling with his pair of wings, he managed to return to the vacuum. He, for the first time, blasphemed Yahweh and his power. He complained about the powerful key that Yahweh had to control heaven; he called it "disgrace", opposing the word "grace", which implied to the inhabitants of heaven "gifts received from Yahweh."

After Lucifer flew madly through the vacuum, he gradually realized the absence of the strong compressed pressure that previously bothered those who flew there. His eyes went back to perception, making him see again, and when that happened, he opened them wide and found that the vacuum had turned into a charming place.

The space recently designed and created by Yahweh made Lucifer feel the freshness of the pleasant wind; he, now, having nowhere to go, was lost to wandering in the immensity of the intense blue.

Yahweh was in a place of immense space and felt the need to

lean on something concrete, like his pinnacle. Since it was all formless and empty, only filled with the immeasurable deep blue, he realized carefully that by surrendering the vacuum to the wind, the wind, in all its potentiality, had transformed everything into radiant energy. The intense blue was nothing more than a shock caused by the passage of an electric current that could make everything move free. The first result of this exuberant energy was to become the compressed and humid space, which gradually gained consistency and conditions to evaporate into gray mass. Yahweh tried it and saw it to be a solid mass, capable of becoming liquid, without color, smell or taste, which flowed from space without any obstacle, called it water. He made the water abundant over the solid parts of the masses, and leaning on the heights, he admired the congenital mixture of liquid and solid masses. He noted that the deep blue had turned a pale color, mingling with a mist suspended in the layers of the atmosphere. Yahweh found all this very good.

Lucifer, although he did not know that Yahweh was present in one of the dimensions of this immeasurable space, he experienced innocuous changes there. He, who once wandered from corner to corner, was able to rest quietly on the solid parts of the mass divided between liquids and solids. Faced with these inexplicable phenomena, he thought of the following hypothesis: "If everything here is suddenly changing, surely the Creator would have to be somewhere in this space." He flew fast through space hoping to find Yahweh somewhere, creating things in that immeasurable place, as he had done in heaven.

Lucifer, strolling wildly through space, could finally see Yahweh subjected to one of those immeasurable places building all the new through the imperious evocation of his magnificent words. He thought of approaching Yahweh and sinisterly teasing him to disrupt his plans, but he held back with the brilliant idea of settling on the solid parts of the cold, wet masses and watching Yahweh create everything. This idea became for him an expectation of a winding path. He thought, "I will observe him in all his creation and discover the power of his making things exist; in this way I will return to Heaven and make the Almighty there!" He stood still, watching Yahweh shape that immeasurable place.

Yahweh observed that the waters were shapeless without order; solid parts sometimes crumbled in the vehemently wind, becoming excessively liquid and slippery. He needed to investigate all the space and for that, it was necessary to make the light exist there. He thought of bringing the rays of light from the throne, but as he was facing another creation, he preferred to give the space its own light. Then he firmly snored, "Let there be light!"

In addition, in a fascination, light began to exist with the emergence of a radiant star made up of its own energetic existence. Yahweh seeing that this star held steady his light, applied by his own energy, called it the Sun and made it slowly rotate through space, scattering light where there was none.

Sunlight refracted between the waters and the air, producing for Yahweh a subjective sensation of enormous liveliness resulting in a mixture of infinite colors, like a luminous energy. Yahweh saw that the light was good, and as it came from that body, which He called the Sun, blessed it as coming from a divine star of his creation.

Lucifer, who saw part of the space in blue and gray, suddenly came across the multifaceted lights in the space. He was dazzled and, even more confused, because he saw the Lord, but could not hear his speech that caused strange and endless changes beneath the sky. He thought, "Where would be by force of Yahweh to enforce his plans? I, Lucifer, will have to discover this force emanating from enchantment." He set his sights on discovering the mysteries of Yahweh and possibly becoming as powerful as he did.

The sun, turning around space, caused the solid parts of the mass to melt, making them uncontrollably liquid. The wind tried to temper the heat and the cold, but it did not reach the necessary balance. All mass became liquid and the waters swelled in disorder, becoming hot, boiling. In observing this strange phenomenon,

Yahweh realized that the sun should not endure over space, since his energy did not provide an efficient structure, befitting the influence of the wind, causing him to shake roughly. He thought of destroying the sun, but not everything created from it should ever be undone; then he simply ceased the sun, raised it in the form of a lamp in space, causing the stormy waters to calm and cool. This took time and as the waters calmed and cooled, he brought forth a solar nebula and a discoid mass of dust and gas from the remnant of the Sun. When the mass melted and cooled to a solid crust, Yahweh stepped on her and felt her steady. In addition, seeing that place, thanks to the Sun, had become a firm and secure crust, he, intending to unify the whole place, assuredly said, "Make the soil!" He made the ground and it gave firmness to all space. Yahweh traveled all over space and experienced it again, treading firmly on some parts of the crust or soil. Due to the sensation he felt, He gave the ground the meaning of ground, because it is shallow and low. He made the ground finite and mysterious, causing the water to get under it, so that the sun did not turn all space into water. Then He again made the sun strong and soon realized that the newly created ground had become bitter in order to make unexplained cracks, becoming imperfect, before His eyes. Yahweh therefore had another brilliant idea. He created the trajectory of one star around another, a kind of gravitational action called a solar orbit. With this procedure, the sun and the ground would keep their distance from each other, maintaining an important dependency line between them. Yahweh later realized that the ground had become a pleasant place and that the waters, wind, and sunlight were doing so. The floor stretched like a flat carpet, mixed with sunlight and resulting in various colors reflected and absorbed throughout the identifiable parts of immeasurable space. Soil, sun and space all came together. Because of this splendid composition, Yahweh's attention was turned to the soil, and by shedding some of the water into it, forming an ocean, he effectively says that the soil would be called earth,, defining it as a soft part of the soil capable of produce things.

The wind blew the drifting ocean waters so that they would again flood the earth, being completely flat. Yahweh saw that he would have to contain the waters, and thus made the earth high, giving rise to hills, valleys and mountains.

When the waters were contained or mapped, the land became a vast territory, surrounded by them. The splendor of the colors made the earth and all infinity stand out in a dazzling way, and from Yahweh's view, the monochromatic radiation drew his attention to the green color. He studied this color closely and, seeing the earth in its full form, saw that the green color would be the color of balance; He brought this color with new ideas for the continuity of the project.

Yahweh took the color green, materialized it, turned it into dust, and threw it into the ocean, saying, "Make the sea plants!"

Because the waters of the ocean were made up of two hydrogen molecules, linked to one oxygen molecule, an algae mat appeared in the ocean. Algae soon prospered and gave rise to new and all-aquatic plant species, such as a dazzling green garden. Although Yahweh liked this creation in his project, he soon realized that algae and aquatic plants kept spreading among the waters. To solve this serious problem, He would give rise to some species capable of stopping the excess of algae and aquatic plants without devastating them. Faced with this delicacy, in order to preserve what was instituted in the ocean, He said: "May the marine animals emerge, each one according to its species!"

Yahweh created the animals of the marine species, controlling them through the food chain. Each animal would feed or feed the other, in addition to providing itself with algae and all species of existing aquatic plants, keeping the new habitat in perfect balance.

The ocean was filled with aquatic animals of all created species: fish, crustaceans, coelenterates and sponges. Yahweh observed that animals restored the balance of the ocean and that aquatic life was another kingdom. He thought it was very good.

The Earth relied on the Sun and the immense ocean full of life, but even so, due to its measurable vastness, - which it also seemed, it could never be measured - came from more projects. Then, seeing Yahweh that the water kept evaporating from the ocean, sometimes making a thick fog cover the Earth, leaving it, sometimes gray and dark, he thought of creating more things.

Yahweh harvested the colors of the sunlight, decomposed them into various colors, and transformed them into dust, giving origin to the seeds. He threw the seeds in the wind, saying: "May these seeds make grass, herbs and trees sprout from the soil and that each one, according to its species, produce flowers, fruits and seeds to perpetuate itself". The effect was fantastic; the seeds fell all over the Earth and generated vascular plants and plants with seeds in all their species. Yahweh watched them sprout, grow and reproduce flowers and fruits. He thought it was very good.

Yahweh, looking at the immense space, came to Him the remembrance of the heavenly angels. He thought of creating angels to fill the earth and fly over everything that existed in it, including through outer space. But angels, He thought, were created for Heaven and there would be other kingdoms to be instituted on Earth. Then, He, paying homage to the heavenly angels, said in a strong tone, inspired by joy: "May the earth produce birds, according to the species of each one. And the earth became moved with the appearance of all species of birds, all with wings, like those of angels, some being able to fly; others, non - runners, aquatic, raptors or raptors. Yahweh wanted all types of birds to live and fly according to their species and their limits. In observing the birds within their physical and geographical conditions favorable to their survival, He found everything very good.

Lucifer insisting on knowing "where would be the strength of Yahweh to make his plans emerge", as soon as the Creator sowed the seeds all over the earth and they generated the plants in all their species, sprouting, growing and reproducing flowers and fruits, he took advantage of them to serve as hiding places. Sneaking behind the trees, he approached Yahweh and, remaining ecliptic, watched him create things. Every new thing that appeared in the new kingdoms created by Yahweh left him more suffering. He observed everything and felt an enormous sadness when he realized that it was not happening, before the eyes of his Creator, of a vassal, which would imply that his glory was only borrowed. He, realizing himself clearly, to be his role for reflection on the infinite majesty of Yahweh, who had given him the courage of life, did not conform. He hid behind the trees and, becoming confused in the sunlight, he became invisible, capable of not feeling his presence there.

Yahweh, busy with his new projects, was not aware of the presence of Lucifer, there, elliptical, behind the trees, spying on him.

Yahweh, after raising birds of all sizes and species, observed the plants and how much they grew and gave flowers, fruits and seeds, then, seeing the need to moderate them to excess, he decided to raise the animals, each according their species, vertebrates and invertebrates, offering physical and geographical conditions favorable to their survival. After everything was very organized, He saw that everything was good.

Yahweh observed the whole earth and also the sun gravitating on it and realized that although it was all good, it would still have to decrease the power of the sun, which, due to the intense rays, still seemed to harm the earth and all living beings that they inhabited. He then looked at the firmament and saw that, just like the Earth and the Sun, He could give life to other stars, each with its own characteristic, becoming one dependent on the other, in terms of general consolidation.

Then He studied the Sun and saw the possibilities for it to distance itself from the Earth and become a source of energy for every being or thing resulting from His creation.

When the Sun distanced itself from the Earth and the Earth began to revolve around the Sun, Yahweh realized that, at one time or another, some parts of the Earth maintained the complete absence of luminosity, this incredible phenomenon, He called it darkness. And seeing, therefore, that the darkness or the absolute lack of light would not do well to the Earth, He made appear in the infinite another star of less luminosity, which was able to revolve around the Earth, emitting light, when some part of it was dark. This star he named the Moon, making it the only natural satellite on earth. Yahweh realizing the Moon and its usefulness to the newly created kingdoms, He thought it was very good and, so good, that he made thousands and billions of stars and so many other mysterious stars appear and everything, everything was dazzling.

Wherever the earth darkened and gained the luminosity of the moon and stars, Yahweh called it night and where on earth it was clear, He called it day. So day and night were done and from that division He realized that he had also created time, being directly linked to the influence of the presence and absence of light. Although there was no time domain in Heaven, Yahweh was not frightened by this, on the contrary, He thought it good to witness on Earth that in some places living beings rested in the light of the Moon and the stars, because in other places, others remained active in the sunlight. This he called continuity, which was also given the meaning of an uninterrupted connection of the parts of a whole.

Lucifer was increasingly frightened to denote the phenomenal appearance of things created there, from his Creator. If he already lived in unrest, from the moment the time was established, he increased it even more, because if the brightness of the Sun made him almost invisible; that of the Moon made him turn into a gloom and, due to these mutation processes, he would have to be very careful not to be noticed by Yahweh, especially at those times, when he believed he was about to discover one of His mysteries. This mystery seemed to involve the affirmative discourse of its Creator.

Yahweh, observing the Earth, with all its primacy, realized that in some parts of its solid surface it lacked water. Although the sea was, in some parts of the Earth, open, high, continental and coastal, it was not possible to water it completely. He then caused the water on Earth to move continuously according to a cycle of evaporation and transpiration, causing the plants to receive moisture through a catalytic process, strengthening their photosynthesis. He thought it was very good the result.

Yahweh also thought of creating a link between the animal and aquatic kingdoms. To establish this connection, He made the animals also depend on water, and, seeing that the sea was divided into four parts extensively and that this would result in a difficulty for certain animal species to move to him, therefore proposed another creation, that of rivers. He chose thousands of strategic points on Earth and made cracks on these points, so that the fresh and crystalline waters sprout, forming rivers, waterfalls and waterfalls, as well as lakes and ponds. He also placed several species of aquatic animals and plants under these water sources.

When looking at the rivers through the infinite it was possible to see that they met each other, gaining new forms and volumes, sustaining the entire Earth and beings existing on it, diluting, in the end, the minerals present on the terrestrial surface and flowing into the sea, making -the saline.

The vacuum was nothingness and nothingness became immanent made up of everything that exists physically: the totality of space and time and all forms of matter and energy. And as everything came to be contained in one, Yahweh called this invention the Universe or Cosmos, considering the set of Heaven and Earth; two places, to Him, purely concrete.

And Yahweh stood at the center of the Universe to admire him. As an observer, He was faced with all the greatness he had built: the Sun, the Moon, the little stars, the stars, the Earth and all the details made up on it. He thought it was very beautiful and very good.

As Yahweh fixed his eyes on the birds, he remembered his angels and thought how beautiful the Earth would be if they existed on it. He was hesitant to think about the possibility of transferring some of his angels to Earth, making it habitable for them, making them go through the same processes tolerable to birds, plants and animals, but, however, He preferred to preserve the angels in heavenly heights and to give rise to the creation of something whose creature could place above others that he had created on earth. When thinking about giving existence to this creature to dominate everything and everything that was on Earth, he thought of a strong being, capable of thinking and acting for himself, but, unfortunately when thinking about Lucifer and all his ambiguity, he felt a little frustrated and decided to observe the Universe more, traveling between galaxies and giving rise to so many other things which would become eternally mysterious.

CHAPTER 4

THE CREATION OF HUMANS

Yahweh carefully reexamined the Universe and everything in it, and when he encountered the Earth again, he examined it in detail. Everything He saw on earth, He liked it, but He continued in his mature presentiment that it was still necessary to create for her a creature situated above everything that existed on it. What would it be? He thought of the superiority he had attained in making his angels exist in Heaven and given them important tasks to care for his divine and eternal creation. On Earth there would also be higher beings, capable of taking care of it in a process of direct and simple execution. He thought of putting some angels without wings on them, with strength, strength of mind, courage and vigor, so that they would inhabit the Earth and be able to take care of everything that existed on it. However, he did not hesitate and looked at the land, entering his eyes inside her. He, perceiving her as red and wet, placed himself at the edge of a huge lake and thought about creating a being that would represent the deified cosmos. He humbly touched the earth, took out a piece of clay and kneaded it between his hands, molding and shaping one of his heavenly angels. He analyzed the silhouette of art and, seeing it very identical to his angels, molded it again, changing some characteristics, making it its image and likeness. He satisfied with his art and knowing that the Earth was upright or "hardened", before the mass dried up, He blew the statuette's nostrils lightly and filled it with the Holy Spirit, making it alive. By placing the figurine on the floor, moving, He analyzed it and seeing his project consist of creating a superior being to take care of all and everything that he had created on Earth, He made him grow into a stature of 2, 0 meters and, as his art had been made of clay from the humus, Yahweh said: "I gave rise to a new being superior to everything I created and it will also be up to him to remove the earth and make it perpetuate his species and your own food. Therefore, because he was created from the dust of the earth and became responsible for her humus, I will call him a man; man of the red earth, reminding him to always be my creature born of the earth".

In affirming this, Yahweh gave the newly created man of the land the insight and made him walk and know everything on earth. The man wandered alone among the fields and the woods and watched everything around him and slept when the sun gave way to the moon's glow and did nothing, because the other creatures were different from him and he had no one of similarity or discernment to communicate.

Yahweh seeing man alone as a wanderer, observing everything and not being able to share anything with anyone who existed, according to his likeness and discernment, He remembered that for every living species, He had made male and female for the perpetuation of their species. The same He would do to the newly created and evaluated man, according to his criteria.

He then made the man from the red earth to lie down on the grass and fell asleep. Using it as a mold he made another figurine, giving it more delicate aspects, because it would be like the fertile soil, capable of receiving the seed and germinating in its bowels the children of the earth. And by molding all the silhouettes of the delicate figurine, He gave him a slightly more complex internal and external anatomy, making it opposite to man. In his womb, He composed a uterus, called a matrix and connected it to a slit, which would be extended to man to make it fertile, and, to celebrate this, He gave her a cycle of hormonal changes, which was called menstrual. And he said: "You are also my image and likeness and I made you a woman to be a companion to the man. You will become the mother of all mankind, and therefore you will become fertile able to bear children of the earth in your womb. At each interval of time your belly will give you the sign of your fertility. If it has not been fertilized, you will spill your blood on the earth, like the mud that flows by the watershed".

When he finished creating the woman, Yahweh returned to the man and gave him a key and an internal complexity in his reproductive system, capable of fertilizing the woman and generating children on the land.

When giving the woman the height of 1.80 meters, Yahweh blew his nostrils and made her alive. Then He woke the man up and introduced him to his mate. The two humans opened their eyes, sat on the grass and looked at the Creator with resignation.

Two opposing beings were born from the archetype generated from the earth: man and woman. These beings were called the class of humans, which, for Yahweh, would imply their nature and condition: love; understanding; kindness; obedience, fidelity, and, finally, integrity.

And seeing that the Earth is extensive, Yahweh used as a prototype the newly created couple of humans to raise other couples; modifying each individual's features, from appearances, characters, characters and temperaments. By multiplying them, He distributed them to various places on Earth.

The distribution of human couples on earth was done in social groups according to the same ethnicity, so that they lived in community and shared the same language and customs.

Yahweh had given animals and plants the distinction of the reproductive system, its contrasts and their interactions, which he called this sex behavior and also gave it to men and women so that they could interrelate, be fruitful and multiply by filling and submitting their generations to the earth.

Yahweh created humanity, giving it as a reward for its benevolence, making it capable of dominating everything that existed on land, at sea and in the air. In this way, said Yahweh: "I made men and women arise from the dust of the earth, consisted of them the internal and external differences of their bodies, making them opposed beings to unite, become fertile and multiply, filling and submitting to the land".

After Yahweh saw the newly created men and women, each couple taking their place on earth, He thought it was very good.

Again, Yahweh seeing the Universe and, again, looking at some particularities, he observed space and all the stars: the planets and all forms of matter in it, including the Earth and all the elements composed in it. After his meticulous contemplation, He, the supreme and perfect Being, Creator of all things, realized that the solar system would imply in the human universe time as a physical greatness, measured from the Sun and the Moon. He called it day and night.

As Yahweh existed outside the realm of time, when he studied the set of norms to which the universe emanated, He realized that all moving beings on Earth should rest to relieve tension and become more peaceful, setting the day for activities on Earth and nights for rest or rest. The Universe itself would remain constantly working on its movements of rotation and translation. With the rotation movement, the Earth would rotate around its axis, giving the succession of days and nights; the translation would be that of the time it would take the Earth to give a complete turn to the Sun, giving, as the succession of years. In this way, Yahweh created, under the cousin of the rotation movement, the moving beings, sleep, suspending their consciousness and the reduction of sensitivity during the night.

When seeing the men and their due companions, in every corner of the Earth, Yahweh said: "I will not present myself to them as Creator and I will not demand veneration from them. They are below Heaven and everything on Earth must be worked on by them. They are endowed with intelligence, conscience and reason to endure all adversities and acquire all knowledge through practice. As I created the Universe, according to the rules of my perfection, for a long time I will not return to Earth; I will rest and then schedule the right time to return, review it and everything it institutes. Thus, when I return here, I will notify the transformation of everything and everyone, because I will leave here, subjects, transforming beings, each thing will be responsible for another; an established link that everything will be linked in everything ".

Yahweh checked the sun and the moon and remembered the day he started his creation there. He satisfactorily resolved to bless everything and everyone in the Universe. And to extend his blessing, He visited three high hills, composed of rocky stones and very rare vegetation and chose one of them to carry out the blessing. He did so, allowing his voice to reverberate throughout the Universe, being projected through the echo in the three mountains: "I bless all my creation in this Universe, in which I created in extension to Heaven. To prove my faith over everything what I created and liked, I will give the possibility of everything that has life and inhabits the Earth, the air and the sea, to act according to the own will of each species to perpetuate itself, limiting itself to the laws and norms beginning in Heaven " .

In saying this, the mountain on which Yahweh stood, smoked like a furnace, trembling greatly, and when it stopped smoking, a rose plant was born in all of it, which was called burning parsley.

Yahweh left his mark on that mountain and made it, geographically, to keep guarded, becoming an uninhabited, deserted place, to become a meeting place for him with the Universe and, exclusively, with the Earth.

Yahweh, after blessing the Universe, observed everything again and when he saw a couple of humans walking among a beautiful garden, which he had reserved for his rest, he realized that they were the first couple created by Him and that had served as a prototype for the creation of all the other couples scattered in various regions of the Earth. When he saw them soberly, he said: "To this couple, the prototype of my human creation, I will make them live in a wonderful plain, where there will be plenty in abundance for all their generations. I will focus on my promise of commitment to the Universe and the Earth".

He blessed the prototype couple of his human creation and

transported him magically to the promised plain, providing him with the process of perpetuating his own substance and nature, from which, He had created the Universe and all its beings. Proceeding in the same place, Yahweh, before retiring to sleep, looked at the infinite and as if speaking to the whole Universe, said in a loud and firm tone: "I will leave for my rest and when I wake up I will return to my throne and only I will return to this place when the couple of humans, sent to the abundant plain, reach their twenty-first generation and that will imply, when I return, to observe the Universe in all its fullness, balance, protection and stability. Within that period, my entire creation on Earth will be established by its own evolution. The entire material world around humans will be under the aegis of Nature, which is the essential and innate quality for the course of things constituted by me".

The word Nature, given by Yahweh, was restricted to the innate essence about the course of things and the Universe itself, everything connecting in everything and everything, so that the evolution of the physical universe was uninterrupted. Nature would imply a process of construction and reconstruction, given in a patient, confidential and silent way, as if his hands were perpetually touching everything and everyone that existed in the Universe, without distinction or privilege to any beings, things or species. Everything that He had just created would enter into an eternal process of movement, executing its own dynamics. Although He was timeless, he made the Universe a time-measuring clock, which would invisibly mark and adjust the seasons to the exact position of the equinoxes and solstices, in addition to periodically attaching themselves to living beings, according to their biological needs. Nature would become the great partner of this universal watch, acting according to its hands.

Yahweh, after speaking to the whole universe in his loud and firm tone, became invisible. That garden, being a mysterious and peaceful place, would serve Him to rest. Then He set up a soft bed under the crown of a leafy tree, lay down on it and, when he smelled the pleasant smell of substances of different origins that existed in that garden, he fell asleep peacefully. He, however, being a totally timeless Being, his rest, there, in that garden, would be immeasurable to the time of the Universe.

Lucifer hiding behind a leafy tree, somewhere on Earth, heard the invocation of Yahweh's blessing to the Universe from the echo and almost did not believe it when he heard "that all that has life and inhabits the air, the earth and the sea, would act according to the will of each species, to perpetuate itself, according to the gifts of Nature ... "and that He" would return there when the prototype couple of humans reached their twenty-first generation".

Lucifer observed that the word generation would be a degree of affiliation of all living beings created by Yahweh. He would give the power of existence to all living beings on Earth, through the right to other copies of them and, these copies, certainly, would be his offspring, who, successively, would generate others and more others, until the whole Earth was, increasingly inhabited by all its living species. He replied: "Would the Earth be greater than Heaven? Yahweh conferred powers to all animate beings, through the spirit, to the reproduction of their own species"?

Lucifer, thinking that Yahweh had retired to rest on his throne, in the pinnacle of Heaven, stopped hiding and scrutinized some flat regions of the Earth. He intended to meet the prototype couple whom Yahweh had sealed the promise to have him generate his copies until the twenty-first affiliation. He was thinking of some evil plan against the couple, but nevertheless, finding him nowhere, he found himself forced to give up the idea. But he, flying freely from one place to another on Earth, watched her admiring everything, everything that existed on it. During the nights, the outer space left him even more dazzled and as much as the hatred he felt for the power of the creation of Yahweh, something at the heart of him focused on giving him the certainty that the Creator was indeed perfect in your entire creation.

Lucifer, thereafter, taking advantage of the absence of

Yahweh, strolled through the entire space and fully explored it; strolled across the Earth and explored it fully. As he climbed a high hill on Earth, he finally celebrated an impressive discovery. After observing Yahweh becoming the whole vacuum in the Universe, he was convinced that all the power of the Creator would be in the firmness of the word, in the reasoning, in the reason, and that for him to become also powerful, it would be enough to do the use of the imperative tone, expressing, however, his will.

Lucifer, happy, due to this discovery, became even more presumptuous and convinced of his many and rare qualities. He thought coldly: "I do not see my Creator over all that He created; certainly, He must have reached the end of the whole creation of this kingdom and departed for Heaven. There, I will be next to Him and will also show him my power".

Lucifer, made to a sphere of fire, flew quickly across the Earth to see if he was meeting with Yahweh somewhere in it, resting. He, finding no Yahweh anywhere on Earth, became convinced that he would find him in Heaven. He spread his huge wings and flew. When he gained the infinite blue and was confused with the bright sunlight, he magically disappeared in a nebula.

Upon reaching Heaven, Lucifer flew directly to the pinnacle, where Yahweh's seat was, but again, the present light from the throne caused another tremendous shock. Although he did not suffer blindness this time, he noticed that Yahweh was absent from Heaven and, in due course, decided to travel through the three infinite levels to start a rebellion against the Creator.

Lucifer, cunningly, flew to the second level, where the cherubim angels lived and, rightly, addressed the leading cherub. He intended to confess to him about his plans to make an uprising against the Creator and win him sympathy for the adherence to his plans. By bringing the leader of the cherubim up to date with his plans, he gained the necessary trust and sympathy. Lucifer's persuasive speech boiled down to the following argument: "Rebellion would be good for Heaven and for all angels, seraphim and cherubs, for Yahweh demeans power to all heavenly angels, becoming only He, the omnipotent."

The leader of the cherubim, without measuring consequences, let Lucifer be persuaded and joined his rebellion. He also showed, at his core, the desire to rule Heaven and that is why he found the idea of Lucifer very interesting.

Like Lucifer, although he did not let himself be seen, the leader of the cherubim angels and other celestial angels also envied Yahweh and, due to this malnourished feeling, everyone aspired to possess more relevant hierarchies in Heaven.

The leader of the cherubim, thinking of taking advantage of the situation created by Lucifer, inevitably allowed him to be persuaded, joining him and allowing him to meet there with all the cherubim angels of his hierarchy.

Lucifer, when meeting with the cherubim angels under the support of their leader, made his speech in defense of power as a good for all and some of the cherubim, too, allied themselves with him and their leader.

Lucifer and the leader of the cherubim invited the new allies to disperse from the second level and follow them to the third. All those who adhered to Lucifer's persuasion, accepted the invitation and left the third level. At this lower level, the newly opposed to the creator also met with the messenger angels and executors of the order to persuade them of their convictions against Divine Power.

Lucifer, on this third level, praised the angels in all his works and tried to make them believe that the power that Yahweh had, above all and everything should also belong to them, so that no one in Heaven would need to carry out orders in bondage regime.

Some messenger angels and executors of the works of Yahweh were also convinced of Lucifer's speech and, dreaming of becoming also powerful, joined him to face a long battle.

Lucifer united the persuaded angels of the two spheres and, with them, left for the upper sphere to continue the favorable posture of his idea of upheaval against the Creator. In the upper sphere, although Lucifer made a convincing speech about power, his competence, authority, faculty and all his set of permissions, he was unable to win any adherents.

The seraphim, important inhabitants of the upper spherical field, realized in Yahweh's infinite wisdom that that Lucifer's action was circumstantial and there was no reason to be. They argued, defending themselves: "Only Yahweh is the supreme and perfect Being, Creator and Father of all things, to Him we owe everything to who we are and what we have". Lucifer replied with an ironic tone: "And they will continue to be what they are, merely angels! Because, united with me, they can become powerful angels, capable of dominating everything that belongs to the Creator".

The seraphim hid their faces between their wings and were silent. Lucifer belonged to new arguments, but they were useless. He ended up giving up and, meeting with all the orders of converted angels, he fled with them to a place in Heaven, which extended to the northern sides of the lower landing. In that place of Heaven, he, without the Creator's permission, made his home dark and cold.

Lucifer, dragging the angels to the chosen place to the north of the lower landing, subjected them to their dominions, harshly chaining each other. From then on, he wanted everyone to do his own thing. Under his whims, the organized phalanx would act illegally against all Yahweh's concepts. He said to the phalanx, "I will rise above the pinnacle of Yahweh, I will exalt my throne, and I will sit on the mount of the congregation on the northern sides."

Lucifer and his phalanx spent time making daggers with long, sharp blades to wage war in Heaven against Yahweh's legion. He did not tire of reasoning with the phalanx, saying that he was the king of armies and that the angels of Yahweh, of any order, would never defeat them. Gradually he gained omnipotence and felt himself to be all-powerful, capable of devastating the entire kingdom of Yahweh and building his glory in him by overvaluing the evil he would act against divine right and justice.

Lucifer wrote on a huge crystalline slate the meaning of the word evil, discerning it as the opposite of good, that is, everything that opposes virtue, honor and morals. He taught his phalanx that virtue was somewhat dangerous, since it would imply in Yahweh the moral qualities, such as temperance, modesty, generosity and justice, which made all the angels of all the hierarchies of Heaven obey him and fall into eternal servitude, becoming all dominated by Him. He argued: "As for honor, a principle of conduct based on ethics, to which honesty, courage and other behavior considered virtuous, it is also nothing more than a trick of Yahweh to demand servitude from all of us, His creatures; the moral". And he went on to tell the converted angels that the principles of decency, which guided the conduct of individuals and also their moods or moods, were Yahweh's main apparatus for keeping all angels in bondage. And he concluded: "Servitude would be a term used for anyone who was totally dominated by someone and that someone, being the dominator, has every possibility to act according to his own will or autonomy".

Lucifer's lectures on the argument of evil were considered to be the phalanx as a basis for solving all the problems created from that uprising against Yahweh and against the heavenly angels, which did not adhere to his opposition.

Emanuel, invisibly, visited Lucifer's strange place several times and tried with all his strength of deep affection to make the angels, followers of Lucifer's ideologies, repent and free themselves from those chains linked to that horrible link that made them eternal condemned to evil. But the angels, about a third, converted to Lucifer, became weak and, among these conditions, they found themselves eternal prisoners of the king of perversion.

It did not take long for Lucifer to extinguish the ignorant glows of the converted angels and to call them devils, a term he referred to as "mischievous angels", who would henceforth act as oppositional beings to Yahweh and to everything and every creature of Him.

Upon arriving from visits to Lucifer, Emanuel went to the

pinnacle and met with Uriel, letting him know everything that happened in Heaven, especially about Lucifer's atrocious ideas.

Uriel, like Emmanuel, could do nothing, for as long as Yahweh was absent, the only force they should trust would be that of the divine light which seized the forces of Lucifer in favor of defending the Creator's throne.

In the dubious corner of Lucifer, north of Heaven's lower landing, the light from the divine throne had ceased and everything that existed there, from Lucifer's view, was only visible through a gloom. The third of the angels of Yahweh, persuaded by Lucifer, had changed their appearance; their wings went red and their faces, which were sweet and soft, became frightening. Lucifer taught them to have power over themselves in the art of transfiguration, enabling them to form figures or representations of things capable of deceiving others. The word deceit served to induce those close to error, making them easy prey to acts of betrayal, disloyalty and infidelity. Lucifer gradually built up a repertoire of words in his kingdom, building a lexicon opposite to that of Heaven.

CHAPTER 5

LUCIFER'S PERSUASIVE BRAND

When Yahweh woke up in the chaste and pure garden of the Earth, where he rested, he soon revisited the entire Universe and when he settled in the Earth again he realized that the space, in which the stars were located, and that was configured to a great vault over the surface of the Earth, would arouse a special interest to humans, mainly the Sun, the Moon and other visible stars. The entire infinite space region, certainly, would cause fear and, at the same time, enchantment to humans, so that, in time, they would seek science in all its wisdom and knowledge to be located in their proper spaces. In this way, humans would perceive, understand and respect his greatness in all his eternal creation. Reflecting on this, Yahweh once again made his promise to return to Earth when the prototype couple of humans reached their twenty-first generation. After affirming this promise again, He went to Heaven, returning to the pinnacle, where the great angel Uriel, faithfully, veiled the light of his divine throne. Yahweh's arrival in heaven made everything tremble. The light from the pinnacle became strong, spreading its golden rays throughout the celestial kingdom. The messenger angels blew the trumpets and others flew to warn each other about Yahweh's presence. And when everyone heard of the Creator's arrival, they flocked to the pinnacle.

Yahweh, when he reached the pinnacle, sat on the throne, made the light go out and kept his luminescence on. Angels of all orders were at the pinnacle surrounding the divine throne and worshiping Him with sacred reverences. Yahweh thought it was very good and saw that the worship and references made by angels, to Him, it would be an act of deep love and in that would be the basis of his eternal support.

When he saw the angels gathered together, giving him worship and reverence, He remembered when he constituted the plants on Earth, harvesting the colors of the sunlight, decomposing them into various colors, transforming them into dust and giving origin to the seeds. He looked at the angels prostrate before him and spoke to himself: "So, as I created the seeds and spread them all over the earth, so that they germinate and become trees, able to give flowers and fruits and perpetuate themselves and if they also used food for all living beings on Earth, I also feel the need for food and this will come from the glorification of all my creature that I made to inhabit Heaven and Earth. I will call that food, fully spiritual, the bread of life".

Although food was what contains substances that an organism needed to develop and stay alive, Yahweh also felt the need for it. His food would be symbolically, which he would call "the bread of life", implying being like a fiber in which it would contain the strength befitting moral capacity, capable of overcoming difficulties and injustices and solving problems, making decisions firmly, courageously and with dignity. To conclude this symbolic act given to his food, He, right there from the throne, ordered the wind to spread thousands and thousands of small golden seeds in the temperate regions of the Earth, which germinated giving rise to a new species of herbaceous plant known as wheat. And Yahweh said to himself again: "The wheat in the fields will forever remind my angels and they will be cultivated throughout the earth, serving my creatures as staple food. They will serve me as spiritual food, thus representing my eternity. I will nourish my angels with the 'bread of life' and they me with the 'bread of gratitude' and that will be our reciprocal agreement".

The angels, when ceasing worship and reverence for Yahweh, flew in flocks to their respective levels. The angels Uriel and Emmanuel - the latter who could only be seen by Yahweh -

remained on the pinnacle, before the Father's throne.

Emanuel and Uriel reported to Yahweh Lucifer's features and his willing insurrection against the kingdom of Heaven. Yahweh remembered the free will he had given Lucifer, and that, however, gave him the possibility to make decisions following the own discernment, which, if for good, would benefit everyone; if by evil, it would be a misfortune.

Yahweh realized that the fact that Lucifer persuaded a third of the heavenly angels would happen for an evil reason and, before the inevitable rumors would happen, he would have to act with caution. Yahweh knew that Lucifer would have to answer for the incidence of his actions and also explain what value he would expect from those acts. In order to obtain answers to such questions, Yahweh, therefore, would have to go to Lucifer, and as this revolting angel was anointed by His deliberate sentence, nothing serious would happen.

Yahweh, having to visit Lucifer, would again be absent from his throne, so He asked his son Emmanuel, who remained invisible, to visit the third sphere and observe all the messenger angels and executors of his works and, whoever saw him , approach and kneel before him, saying: "The Lord Yahweh is among us all!" bring it to the pinnacle.

Emanuel followed Yahweh's order. He visited the third sphere and as soon as he got there, a messenger angel saw him and came to meet him and kneeled at his feet, enforcing Yahweh's prediction. Emmanuel led the messenger angel, chosen through the Creator's prediction, to the pinnacle.

Upon reaching the pinnacle and going to the throne, the angel knelt before the Creator and made a humble bow to Him. Yahweh welcomed him with joy, making him acquire a new face and making him an important cherub of his order. The messenger angel was renamed Gabriel. Yahweh solemnly blessed him: "I will trust you with an important mission. You will be my eternal messenger, the one who will announce my omens, whether here or elsewhere to be instituted.

Yahweh built a bell jar and a crystal crown, both shiny and made it a home and ornament for the angel Gabriel, affirming it: "I made your home on my pinnacle and also a crown, both decorated with crystal so that you will eternally obtain the physical, vital, emotional, mental and spiritual balance and be worthy to become my angel and faithful messenger".

The angel Gabriel was crowned by Yahweh and then taken to his new home. Emanuel, being invisible on the pinnacle, Yahweh made him visible again and invited him to sit on the right of his throne and, as for Uriel; he was also invited to sit on the left.

Yahweh convinced that he would visit Lucifer and do it again to convert to good, he would have to be absent from the throne. Therefore, as the visit would not be prolonged, He would not leave the divine light on the throne in the custody of the guardian Uriel. He made a huge golden dagger appear in his hands, inserted in a silver-colored scabbard, in which he had engraved the following sentence: "Pax in caelo angelorum!" ("Peace in Heaven to the angels!") And laid her on her throne, without bothering to explain to the angels Uriel and Emanuel why that weapon or the end it was destined for. He simply asked Emmanuel and Uriel to watch over her, and then He left the pinnacle in order to visit Lucifer.

When Yahweh arrived at Lucifer's abode, built north of Heaven's lower landing, He found the place deserted and cold. He found only Lucifer's light to shine on everything and everyone, and that light, why they didn't understand, was totally blinding, causing the atmosphere to be chilling.

For Yahweh, light meant life implying the creation of everything that was perfect and divine and, due to this contrast, He was somewhat shaken, because Lucifer had been one of his great works, a radiant being, in which all its magnificence and not that simple conjuncture.

But Yahweh, although he was certain that he had granted free will to his great angel of light, being in that inhospitable place, decided to help him, thinking Lucifer was going through a torpor or a depressive picture.

Yahweh made his light shine bright and warm, spreading it all over the place of Lucifer. Rumors were heard and wings rustled in protest against the divine light. Yahweh contemplated everything and everyone, in absolute vision, and saw the third of his ex-angels lying face down, blind and trembling due to the light, which had become overblown for them. Yahweh decreased the intensity and heat of the light and Lucifer's angels instantly calmed down.

Lucifer, seated on an ivory throne, which moved quickly from side to side, as if watching all four corners of the restricted city, did not notice, as soon as, being discovered there by Yahweh. He also felt uncomfortable due to the glow that had appeared there, even though it suddenly waned.

Yahweh observed Lucifer's throne and, seeing it above the plane of the converted angels, studied a way on how to approach him so that both could talk to each other. Hence he created another throne identical to that of Lucifer. It made him spin and fly hovering next to his.

The two thrones allied side by side. Lucifer, upon realizing the Creator, was furious, asking him to completely turn off his light. Yahweh completely turned off the light, opting for the weak light of Lucifer. The two plunged into the gloom so that, if they looked down, they would no longer see the angels - or Lucifer's devils - lying face down. Everyone calmed down and hid in the darkness. Yahweh observed this and noticed the weakness of Lucifer's discernment, for there was no comfort there, which He would never subject to his creatures.

After the two thrones lined up side by side and the light of Yahweh went out, Lucifer, still inspired by an inexplicable anger, wanted to know why the Creator's boldness was there, in his city. Yahweh replied, "Everything is part of my creation!"

Lucifer smiled wryly, asking him: "And creation emanates from your power, doesn't it? And he gives you the right to be where you shouldn't be ...”

Yahweh looked at Lucifer and replied: “Power itself does not exist, Lucifer, it is just a pure and natural process of substances necessary for the permanence or support of something capable of leading us to a series of actions. We are all the result of that power”.

Lucifer, thinking that Yahweh wanted to deceive him, muttered subtly: “Power is the faculty of obtaining everything you want for yourself in all its fullness! Yahweh creates everything and everything belongs to Him, even the best place in the kingdom, the pinnacle, built on the highest level, where all his creation, forever, will render him veneration”.

Yahweh remembered the "bread of life" as "bread of the spirit" and replied to Lucifer: "I want my Creatures to have eternal food and, to have it, we need to cultivate the dough so that it never perishes and I, too, want to have my eternal food and I have to do the same. I take care of all my creatures, feeding them with the ‘spirit bread’ and they support me with bliss. Our dough consists of the same bread”.

Lucifer, ignoring Yahweh's speech and belching his inculcated arrogance, said: “I don't know where you want to go, but if you came here to convince me and my devils to return to the celestial spheres, make a mistake! Your throne, although it is in a beautiful pinnacle, is on the same side as mine; both are located to the north; yours, intoxicating and unbearable light and mine half-light, bearable, capable of causing no pain to anyone... ”

It was not difficult to understand the complexity of Lucifer, because, since he left the left side of the throne, due to the result of the choice of the guardian angel of the light, his light was repelled from that of the pinnacle, causing him violent shocks. Certainly, he deserved the penalty of blindness, but Yahweh did not allow this to happen because he was against any kind of imperfection to his creatures. The evil, to which Lucifer refused in the light of the divine throne, was contained within himself: altruism.

Yahweh asked Lucifer why he changed the appearance of the

heavenly angels, who found themselves with red wings and frightening faces. Lucifer only replied: "The same power you have, I also have it and I learned to transform things ..."

Yahweh, indignant at Lucifer's response, warned him: "You cannot create, Lucifer, your power is a persuasive brand, restricted only to changing things, making them the way you want and that is a very big responsibility . I trusted benevolence in you, giving you the power over things created by me, in order not to let them perish, making them perfect; but you have not restrained yourself in the precepts of my ethics ".

Lucifer seemed frightened to learn of the Creator that he did not possess the power of creation and only that of persuasion. Unfortunately, this would imply that he could not create anything, but censor what would be created, transforming things into new forms. However, he would have to accept that he was a being arising from the creation of Yahweh, and the whole creation was linked to its Creator. Then, wanting to prove to the Creator about his power, he replied: "Power is in the supremacy of imperative discourse and this I discovered when I saw him creating things ..."

Yahweh was surprised to hear this revelation from Lucifer and asked him: "Did you learn to have the power by seeing me creating things"?

Lucifer, fearing to reveal his stay in the universe, on the sly, watching Yahweh give origin to things, made a bad face and replied, lying: "Yes, when I sat at the right of your throne, I witnessed freely everything you did, even when you agreed to put my plans for creating the three levels into practice. I took advantage of every moment to uncover the incidence of your power and discover it; therefore, I also have it".

Yahweh, in addition to being surprised by the revelation of Lucifer, decided to incite him: "So, Lucifer, do you think that power is a simple trick that I use?"

Lucifer replied with a slightly ironic tone: "Not that it would be a trick, but an ingenious resource for creating things emanating through speech..."

Yahweh knowing that power really emanated from discourse in all its manifestations, and that this discourse would acquiesce or abide by a high level of virtue or sanctity, which he himself did not know how to express; he looked at Lucifer and continued the incitement: "Prove to me, Lucifer, all of your creative power and if you are able to create something, I will give you all and all of my creation and I will subject myself to being your vassal for oath of eternal faith".

Lucifer smirked: "This is easy! See, therefore, that I transformed this place into a gloom, configured your angels in a new form and chained them in my own way". Yahweh smiled and replied calmly: "To create is to exist from nothing. What you did Lucifer was to transform what already exists ... even the chain you attached the angels to was not your creation, because it comes from a link, a connection that I proposed between me and all of my creation, you just materialized it for your own benefit, perverting my idea. I know that I must not try my creation, or they me, but I ask you to create something new before my eyes, so that I can fulfill promise made".

Lucifer snorted a blaze of fire and configured himself to be an image of a noble angel closed his eyes and shouted, making his long sentences to the imperative: me the owner of everything! " When he opened his eyes, he saw nothing happen. However, he presumed to be in the same place, but Yahweh realized how much Lucifer had been bewildered. His speech of long sentences to the imperative gave more to arrogance than to arrogance. Because of this, Lucifer found it difficult to build up his desires. That way, the essence of things to be instituted would never be exhaled from him. Power did not involve authority, but the control of desires, which would spring from the core of being to full realization. Also observing how Lucifer tried to metamorphose things for the benefit of him, Yahweh tried to calm him down, seriously warning him: "Power is not in the transformation, Lucifer. The power is in the creation! You are a transforming being, equal to all beings created by me; the only difference is that I gave you the best of everything I could give to my creatures, I made you my seraph, the seal of my perfection, full of wisdom and beauty, but you surprised me with your sense, refusing to participate in my plans and showing you proud, arrogant and boastful. I did not admit to losing you and I wanted to make you my beloved son, to whom I could place all my trust and admiration and you have become weak and cowardly, to the point of acting out of conformity with eternal norms. In this way, I was forced to choose another angel, give him my image and likeness and bless him as a beloved son and eternal son. Therefore, I am still able to prove to you all my love; I will give you time to reflect and repent of all that you have done and, if you do so, you will be able to return with the angels to the place of bliss and everyone will take their places to their proper positions. Otherwise, Lucifer, I will not choose another choice, but to make the brightness of my light go out of you, for I see how confused you are, and all your discernment is divided between good and evil. If you suffer that loss, you will have to subject yourself to seek your own light and all your discernment, unfortunately, will incline to evil. Remember, then, that when you lose the light I have given you, by my grace, you will have only yours. Your discernment, then, may not be good for you from now on. As for the possibilities of transformation, everything will depend on your limits and remember that: transformation is not a power given exclusively to you, but also to all living beings of my creation and this I will call conscience, implying the ability to judge what is correct and what is not, according to moral values and knowledge".

When Yahweh finished the parole, Lucifer, without wanting to face him, made a loud and perverse noise from his burning and contestable insides. The angels - or devils - grunted then, making a terrible noise all over that place.

Yahweh hoped to cease all the boredom of Lucifer and his devils and, after opening all forms of understanding and conjecture to him, trying to help him return to his origin as an angel of light and continue with great projects in Heaven (and also in the newly created Universe). Lucifer, however, showing disinterest, replied: "I want to be what I can be!"

Lucifer thought that Yahweh deceived him and something hard seemed to hammer his head, saying: "Yahweh still fears that I am powerful!" And on an unexpected impulse, he shouted at Yahweh, asking him to leave.

The Creator took pity on Lucifer and the angels - or devils - but as He carried in him the hope that Lucifer would repent of his malevolence, he turned on his intense light to depart from there.

Lucifer, when faced with the rays of the intense light of Yahweh, covered his eyes so as not to see it and, when he uncovered them, no longer the Creator present there. He made another noise and was matched by the hideous grunts of the devils. He thought it was very good, because for him it was the beginning of a powerful experience. He blasphemed Yahweh, saying: Father and son, the two will lose the throne, power and glory! I will be all-powerful as I sit on the ivory throne." Out of his mind, he saw the perfect darkness of Yahweh, there, on an ivory throne, in his underworld.

CHAPTER 6

THE ARMY OF ANGELS

When Yahweh returned to the pinnacle and sat on the throne, He received the sacred reverences from the magnificent angels Uriel, Gabriel and their beloved son, Emmanuel. When Yahweh looked at the golden dagger, he levitated it and left it suspended overhead, as if creating a field of action there to keep it within the limits of the pinnacle. The golden dagger, when entering orbit, slowly started to rotate around the pinnacle. Everyone there watched the dagger, even though they did not understand why it existed. Yahweh said to the three angels: "I was with Lucifer in his dark and sad song and I saw a third of my angels disfigured and chained to each other tied to his designs. I felt sorry for all of them; however, I can do nothing but wait for an answer from Lucifer, which is weakened, impotent and weak".

Yahweh sat on the throne and was too sad because of Lucifer's vehement attitudes. He could do nothing but, quietly, wait for any sign of an answer from Lucifer. It would be a torment for Him to have to fulfill the promise to remove the divine light from Lucifer, but that, however, would not be unfair, since the light would serve the angel carrying her no more. The divine light that served as a shield for Lucifer had become innocuous, without the power of the force to produce effects that Yahweh intended for him in all his glory.

While Yahweh sat on his throne, thinking of new projects for Heaven and the Universe, Lucifer continued in his song, plotting plans to surprise the Creator and all of His angels. He thought of annihilating whatever existed in Heaven and sitting on the throne of the Creator, becoming the whole powerful, capable of governing the kingdom and configuring it according to its contradictory plans.

Lucifer's angels or devils were in bondage and, in that conflicted place, began to learn evil lessons to raise the wicked to the throne and make him sovereign. They would have the sad fate of becoming eternal slaves of Lucifer; this was due to the fact that they freely adhered to the folly of their own choices.

Lucifer, immersed in his devastating plans, never thought of any answer as to whether or not his possible repentance to Yahweh. Once, the time limit for the reply had expired and, suddenly, Lucifer lost its authentic light, becoming an opaque figure and devoid of all its supremacy and beauty.

Yahweh, observing that Lucifer had not reached the agreement of his repentance and returned to Him with the third of the angels who were ruptured, He, without leaving his throne, transferred the light of Lucifer to a celestial body of the Universe. This body looked like that of a star, with less intensity of brightness than the sun and moon, whose fire was able to be perceived on Earth only at dawn or after sunset. He spoke to him: "This celestial body or small star that I create and fix in the Universe, I will make it eternal. It will not have the brightness of the intensity of the Sun or the Moon; it will be opaque to remind me of Lucifer. All the light I gave him and I took from him to donate to this star will deceive the darkness, because it will never be a sustainable light for anyone who gets lost anywhere on Earth and trusts in it". And finally, he concluded: "However, all the brightness of Lucifer, like the brightness of this newly created star, will be a mere obfuscation".

Yahweh took the authentic light of Lucifer and transferred it to the newly created star in the Universe. The star or planet, much like a star, similar to Earth, in size, mass and composition, entered orbit in the Solar System. And Yahweh, without observing the star or planet created and orbited in the Universe, saying: "The day that Lucifer repents and returns to me, with his (or mine) angels, I will return to him the brightness of that star and, then, he will again have the domain of good over everything that I created between Heaven and Earth ".

Lucifer in his underworld suddenly suffered a frightening attack. He seemed to say nothing and had difficulty seeing himself. This went on for a while, and after feeling exhausted by these serious illnesses, he fell asleep on his ivory throne. When he woke up, he felt weak and gradually realized that he had actually asked for his divine light. He was frightened, but in his indignation he sustained his anger against the Creator with impetus. The only way he found to conform to this loss was to remember the power of transformation. He could not create, but he could take on a new form for the beings of Yahweh. In his bitter eagerness, Lucifer made his place turn into darkness and when he expelled fire for the wind, he spread it in that place in the form of torches, making it more somber and dark. His devils growled as if translating a sad torment. Lucifer, angrily, ordered the devils to weave a huge network of lozenges and, after completing it, surrounded his entire space. After encircling his underworld with the network of diamonds, Lucifer granted him only the right to enter and leave that place.

Yahweh knew that Lucifer's time had run out and that he no longer possessed celestial light, which had been transferred to the recent Solar System star. This could put Heaven at risk, for Lucifer, in addition to enjoying free will, was also fully aware of his discernment of good and evil, which made him aware of a transformative being. He wanted to conquer the pinnacle, occupy the throne and become the owner of the entire creation of Yahweh. If that happened, it would be the end of a project full of heavenly accomplishments.

Yahweh summoned all the angels to an assembly at the pinnacle. In that assembly He dealt with matters surrounding Lucifer's malignancy. At the end of the assembly, Yahweh made the golden dagger go out of orbit and hover against one of the angels, immobilized above his head. The angels who stood next to the angel with the golden dagger hanging from their heads, turned away from him, frightened. Yahweh said: "This is the angel chosen to keep my dagger and to know how to use it, when possible, in the name of peace and justice".

The golden dagger descended slowly and landed in the hands of the chosen angel. The angel held the golden dagger and fell to his knees, saying: "Let the will of my Father and Creator be done".

Yahweh brought the chosen angel closer to his throne. The angel came and bowed to him humbly. Yahweh blessed him saying: "You were chosen to defend Heaven. You will have my shield as protection. You will be just like me and your mission will be that of commander, guardian and combatant against heresy or opinion contrary to what is accepted in Heaven".

The chosen angel was baptized with the name of Michael due to his humility before the Yahweh and to all the heavenly angels.

Yahweh continued the speech: "You must be careful with this dagger, because it will strike those who are against us. It will also use your strength and discernment to disarm the enemy. I will give you the right to recruit the heavenly angels and to form our army. The struggle faced by our army will be either intended or provided with altruism, envy and hatred and we will therefore not act with violence, but with justice".

At the end of the speech, Yahweh looked steadily at the recent angel Miguel and emphasized: "You, Miguel, will receive all the wisdom and instructions to wield this weapon and lead your army".

The angel Michael prostrated himself before Yahweh, again, humbly thanked him for his trust in the post and then got up, drew the golden dagger and raised it in front of all the angels in Heaven, showing them the endorsement received of the Creator. From there he would form an army of angels in Heaven to refuse Lucifer's evil.

The army equipped by the angel Miguel had thousands of angels, whose corps of troops was called the Celestial Army. Due to the number of angels included in the army, Yahweh made another golden dagger, like Miguel's, and handed it to the angel Gabriel: "You, besides being the angel of the annunciation, you will also have a dagger and you will help the angel Miguel to compose the army of the Celestial Legion ".

Gabriel was deposed from the glass dome he occupied as the official messenger angel of Yahweh and, upon receiving the golden dagger, went to join Miguel. The two talked about how they would constitute the Celestial Army and reached an agreement to divide the army into three large corporations to defend the three infinite levels.

The Celestial Army, in its three corporations, has not failed to perfect itself in combat angels, making them agile and capable of taking mature actions through doctrinal experiments in defense, protection and attack. After lots and lots of training, Miguel observed that the angels of the three corporations also needed to train the combat with the daggers, because, if Lucifer also used them with his army, everyone would run the risk of being annihilated. He and the angel Gabriel went to the pinnacle to ask Yahweh for permission for the soldiers of the three corporations to also use the daggers, each having a copy of them. Yahweh, not wanting to make use of the violence, rejected Miguel and Gabriel's request.

Lucifer, wanting to take revenge on Yahweh, felt the need to start acting quickly. He recruited some of the devils, met with them around his throne, and ordered them to carry out a terrible plan. The devils, possessed by Lucifer's mischievous spirit, hurried to carry out the tricky action. They flew in flocks to the third level of Heaven and invaded it. The messenger angels sounded their trumpets and brought the combatants of the third corporation of the Celestial Army into action.

Lucifer's battle against the fighters of the Celestial Army's third corporation was a terrible one. As Lucifer's army had the power of transformation, some devotees took on the form of terrible monsters and ended up leaving unscathed. They made use of terrible sharp daggers and annihilated a few hundred angels from the third level and, at the end of the battle, took with them, as hostages, seven angels, four of the messengers and three of the executioners of the order.

One of the executing angels of the order, seeing the fighting combatant angels of the third corporation of the Celestial Army annihilated, wept sadly and his tears flowed among the dead soldiers. Yahweh sensed something strange happening on his throne in some part of Heaven. He rose from the throne, left the spire and quickly visited all the levels of Heaven. Upon reaching the third level, he saw a simple executing angel of his order weeping and beside him the bodies of hundreds of mutilated angels. Yahweh understood what happened and gave a strong breath so that the Holy Spirit would descend on the bodies of the dead angels and bring them back to life. The angel, who mourned the death of the other angels in his sphere, wiped his eyes and, sobbing, knelt before Yahweh and said: "Blessed are the Lord our Father and our God who foresaw my pain translated from this throne in this throne worth of tears. Blessed are you, my Lord Yahweh, who restored life to the heavenly angels, who were annihilated by the forces of the evil spirits of Lucifer".

Yahweh girded the angel's forehead, raised him up and said: "You suffered with the dead, because you have them as brothers. You saw what I did and you knew how to thank them for their lives. As of today, you will be incorporated into the Celestial Army and you will be known as Raphael, implying an important statement of what you saw "Yahweh cure". Due to your feeling of pain and solidarity, caused by the misery of others, I will make you the angel of mercy and you will be the intercessor of all the heavenly angels".

Yahweh met with the soldier angels of the three corporations of the Celestial Army and introduced them to the intercessor angel, Raphael. All there, gathered together, heard reports of the angel Rafael about the war caused by Lucifer, in that lower level of Heaven. The angels Miguel and Gabriel looked at each other silently wondering what weapons they would use against the cunning enemy.

Yahweh, being aware of all the details about Lucifer's furtive battle against his third-tier angels and the use of weapons used to annihilate his messenger and executor angels, was too sad.

Yahweh, although he did not want to use violence, when thinking about Lucifer's evil capacity to turn things to his advantage and about the cowardly annihilation done to the angels of Heaven, he called Miguel and Gabriel to the pinnacle and authorized them to do copies of their daggers and distribute them to the soldier angels of the three corporations. Miguel and Gabriel copied their swords and distributed them to the soldiers of the Celestial Army, teaching them how to manipulate them.

Although Yahweh could destroy Lucifer and the third of the perverted angels, He would not. He, therefore, had claimed never to destroy any species of his creation. This, however, made it clear that the only way to destroy something of their creation would happen through transformation, that is, something generated by their own creatures, which, if seen as power, was defined by the following determination: "Each of its creation would have the discernment or the ability to choose its actions, that is, which way to go, even if this is beneficial or not. If Lucifer were to be destroyed it would have to happen through battle. This confrontation, therefore, would be a cause and every cause was based on a principle and that principle, which they were facing, came from a set of conflicting ideas succeeded by Lucifer".

Yahweh defended the good and, in the name of justice and perseverance, he would never want transformation in the kingdom of Heaven, because it generated causes and effects that are often irreparable, perhaps because of this, He said: "I am what I am!" and it made it obvious that whatever He created would be forever what it was; thus avoiding the risk of any debasement.

Lucifer, upon receiving the seven hostage angels on his throne, celebrated by blowing fire and spreading it in great flames throughout the four places of his underworld, while looking at the seven captured angels, he screamed malevolently: "I will have all the angels of the kingdom of Heaven. I, having the power of transformation, will give new shape to everything that suits me. I will make these seven angels a gift to Yahweh! He, even with all his might, will never discover my feat! " In saying this, Lucifer flew among the devils and chose one of them to command his underworld, while he was away.

The devil chosen by Lucifer was the former leader of the Cherubim order, who will allow him to be covered with pride and excessive admiration of himself, likewise Lucifer. He was appointed to a new post invented by Lucifer whose job would be that of the devil. Lucifer conferred it with honor on the new office, giving it the name of Beelzebub. Lucifer did not give Beelzebub any throne, but gave him the order to watch over the entire kingdom and to apply any punishment to those who deserved it.

After naming the ex-cherub who was transferred to the devil and now in devil, called Beelzebub, Lucifer wasted the seven angels, chained them and, in a secret action, took them to the Universe, having as base point the planet Earth.

Upon reaching planet Earth, Lucifer landed with the seven angels chained to a pleasant lawn and sat down and made them also sit on it. In silence, they watched the entire space around them. Later, Lucifer broke the silence by asking the seven angels a question: "Did the great Yahweh tell you about this new world made up of Him, on the sly"?

The angels did not know and did not want to respond to Lucifer, remaining inert and silent. Lucifer repeated the question in a slow and loud tone, and one of the seven angels broke their silence, answering him: "Everything that our Father creates is for bliss. He has the power over everything and does not need to consult us or talk about what he does or does not do..."

Lucifer, upon hearing the commentary angel's comment, flew towards him and slapped him in the face saying: "So, as Yahweh was betraying me, they will also betray you, abandoning you in Heaven and coming to live here. Open your eyes and see that His whole creation in this place is much more splendid than there!"

The seven angels knew the word "splendid", the same thing as "splendor" and that word implied perfection and harmony. They thought: "Everything done by Yahweh is splendid!" They had no knowledge of evil and if Lucifer wanted in his speech to demonstrate to them that the place was more beautiful or better than Heaven, making use of the relative superlative of superiority or inferiority, it had no effect. The seven angels boiled down to everything that Yahweh did as an equality or uniformity. Visions contrary to equality or uniformity, only belonged to Lucifer, because he lived anchored in the evil that came from envy, greed and selfishness, classified by Yahweh as transgression or sin.

Lucifer and the seven angels sitting on the grass watched that little piece of Earth, where plants of all species seemed to form a sacred altar; some bending their branches with fragrant flowers and fruits. Below the sacred altar obviously formed by the plants, a blue lake could be seen receiving clear and crystalline waters drained between the rocks. In this blue lake, besides having several qualities of aquatic animals, on the banks several species of terrestrial and flying animals, small and large, strolled in flocks. Lucifer knew and knew how to distinguish all the sets of species made by Yahweh and introduced them to angels: animals, plants, lakes, rocks, mountains and so on. The whole harmonious scene was the focus of the seven angels, leaving them impressed by that great creation of Yahweh.

Lucifer, after presenting the set of numerous and diverse things on planet Earth to the seven angels, he moved with them to the top of a mountain, making them look down on the plains, plateaus and reliefs. The seven angels were enchanted by everything they saw from the top of the mountain.

Lucifer, although he was cloistered in his bitterness, automatically plunged into his deep ego and watched carefully the whole surrounding scene of that place. He, for a few moments, took the risk of not wanting to know more about wars or strife and to return to peace with the Creator again. Something inside him reasoned, as if the latent conscience at its core made him realize how wrong he was. Something moved him inside, forcibly, reminding him concisely: "Ab aeterno tempore Universarum Deusorum", "Since the time of Almighty God". The silence was interrupted by one of the seven angels singing, due to an alienated excitement of charm, a verse in honor and glory to Yahweh: "Confitemini Domino, quoniam ipse est dominus omnium!" (Give thanks to the Lord, because He is the Lord of all things). The other six messenger angels and executors of the order, in the face of the sudden attitude of one of the angels, who had sung glory to Yahweh, fell on their knees and sang in leather, affirming the song in praise of the Eternal Father: "Benedictus Dominus Deus: Benedictus, qui creavit!". (Blessed be Yahweh! Blessed be all that He created!)

Lucifer, hearing the chants of the seven angels, suddenly became impatient of that place and let himself lose consciousness again ready to come out of latency and come to the fore as an antidote to his spirit. Suddenly, he was transfigured into a monstrous angel, red and poisoned by hatred, looking at the seven angels with an ambiguous look.

The seven angels were surprised to see Lucifer incarnate in the spirit of evil, looking at them normally and everyone raised their hands to Heaven and, unanimously, acclaimed the Lord for mercy. "Misercordia Domine Deus propitius esto!" (O Lord God of mercy has mercy!).

Lucifer, transfigured to terror and stricken by terrible wrath, ordered the seven angels to remain silent and, as he could not, due to their continuous acclamations to the impatient Yahweh, he thought of keeping them chained to the chains and abandoning them on that planet. He reasoned inside, thinking wickedly: "I will leave you here, on this planet out of the sight of Yahweh, who will return here only when His promise fulfills. I will give these seven angels my disenchantment! "

Lucifer understood that, like Yahweh and the angels inhabitants of Heaven, he also lived under the lights of timeless dogma, but to the living beings of the planet Earth everything was measured in a period of time present, past and future, being marked periodically between the duration of the Earth's rotation around its axis and through the revolution of any star in the Solar System around the Sun. The proof of this was in the fact that the period between sunset and dawn, which Yahweh called night and day.

One night, when the phase of the Moon became obscure over the region of the earth where Lucifer and the seven angels were; Lucifer, strangled with rage, released the seven angels from the chain by weaving short soliloquies: "These angels of Yahweh are no longer angels, because I took off their wings!" And he continued: "The Almighty said that I am not able to create, only to transform ... to transform things into others, is it not the same thing to create"? I was indignant, reasoning with the thought: "Yahweh said that to face me before His power... I will give the Creator a terrible answer".

Lucifer thought of transforming the seven angels into things capable of destroying everything that existed on planet Earth. He, however, noticed the four-legged animals and their species tearing and devouring leafy tree branches, laughed and thought maliciously: "If there were huge animals in this place, it would soon be over!" Thinking this, Lucifer noticed a group of reptiles coming out of a heap of rocks, gnawing their belly through the grass and heading towards the banks of the pond. Lucifer followed the reptiles and saw them running, deftly, invented to transform some of them into huge lizards. And in denoting his wickedly strong spirit in adversity against Yahweh, Lucifer looked at the huge reptiles, then at the seven angels and said: "Isn't transforming the same thing as creating? Look what I did; I turned small animals into big ones, capable of destroying everything that Yahweh created on this immense planet! "

The seven angels, reproving Lucifer's features, joined one another in fright. Lucifer, as if enjoying the game, seeing other reptiles, also transfigured them in various sizes.

From this evil of Lucifer, in transforming the delicate lizards into terrible giants, all the moving creatures on Earth would have to suffer terrible impacts when faced with them.

Lucifer, at the end of his transformation to reptiles, called them "terrible lizards" and these became some species that had the bird's hip and others the lizard's hip, some would adapt to land and water; others the land, the water and the air and that for Lucifer seemed very good, because some species would feed on plants and others on meat, guaranteeing a general devastation of everything that existed on planet Earth.

At dawn, Lucifer scattered the terrible lizards to various places on Earth and then took the seven angels to the sea and made them known to him. Lucifer told the seven angels that the sea, although it belonged to the planet Earth, was another world and that other species of animals inhabited it that Yahweh, when creating them, called them aquatic.

The seven angels standing by the sea delighted in the fine white sand and the freshness of the wind and everything, everything that their eyes could reach. All the sudden vision, of that bucolic scene, caused them to desire communion with Yahweh. They seemed, at that moment, to want to give Yahweh adoration, veneration and glorification, because everything they saw and felt was very good and everything was part of the Creator's projects, of which, they also belonged. They, immeasurably silent, looked at the sea and were delighted, because the sea seemed infinite and its water, transparent, changed its color, making it blue, green and even gray.

The wind strongly touched the waters of the sea and they rose, sometimes low and high, causing ripples that dissipated in the flat sand, sometimes between rocks and hills. The seven angels observed that the spectacle of the receding waters of the sea - or the waves - was continuous and its continuity caused enchantment to all who saw it for the first time or many times.

Lucifer realizing that the seven angels, once again, seemed enchanted with this other work of Yahweh, looked at them and said: "Another wonder that I must undo. If they think that Yahweh only creates wonders, I look at that sea and see terrible animals, capable of destroying it! "

In saying this, Lucifer flew quickly, stood up on the high waves of the sea and wandered from side to side, searching the ocean depths. When he returned to the seafront, he addressed the seven angels and said to them: "Look how I am able to create too! Yahweh made aquatic animals too small for this world so vast and so voluminous of water". When pronouncing this, the sea stirred and it was possible to see huge fish of the cetacean specimen which swam in a storm to the point of haunting all the smaller fish.

The seven angels looked at the sea and then shamefully at Lucifer. One of the seven angels, with a radiated aura, approached Lucifer and replied: "Whatever you do, Lucifer, nothing will ever destroy the work of Yahweh, because everything He created is eternal! You are also His creation and as much as you want to destroy it, He keeps you firm! Everything you want to show us as your creation is just a simple transformation or modification of what Yahweh created. You are showing us your imperfection and that is a very sad eternity, because everything that comes in the name of Yahweh is splendid, beautiful and harmonious. He manages to connect everything in everything, so that one thing belongs to the other in solidarity and you are doing everything inside out. However, I warn you not to despise the Divine Creation, because you are also a result of It".

Lucifer was enraged when he heard the angel's impetuous speech. He thought that the angel's intention was to convince him to convert to the good and to make him regret everything he did against the creation of Yahweh. He thought: "Creator enim omnia ex omnibus, ex nusquam, ipsum. Nihil habentes et omnia possentes". (To the Creator, everything comes from nothing, for me everything comes from everything, Him. Having nothing and possessing everything.).

He wanted to be himself and he would never let his feelings change which focused on law and justice. Therefore, wanting to seriously offend the dignity of the seven angels, he transformed them into humans, saying: "They will no longer be heavenly angels, they will never return to the third level of Heaven and they will never see the face of Yahweh again.

They will inhabit the Earth and live among humans, because I transformed their images similar to theirs".

The seven angels looked at each other, saying that Lucifer had changed their outer form. They did not know humans and, therefore, their new face did not frighten them. This behavior was due to the rich fact that, psychologically, they feel the same in the soul, that is, the appearances of humans, but the souls of angels. Lucifer had no discernment capable of affecting them inwardly.

Lucifer thought of introducing the seven newly humanized angels to humans native to Earth, but since the transformation was a clear intention to punish them, he preferred to abandon them on that planet, believing that they had terrible experiences. He then looked at the seven humanized angels and applied another of his wickedness to them, cursing: "From the day you face the human's native to Earth, you will have the same needs as them, you will be thirsty and hungry and they will seek sustenance with their own labor, cultivate the land and take their food from it".

In making this last transformation in opposition to the creation of Yahweh and cursing the accursed speech limited to the greed of humans, Lucifer, at nightfall, transported the seven humanized angels to a dense forest, abandoning them there. He said goodbye to them, saying: "Follow the paths you have to follow and live for yourself, in this vast world, your new experiences. You will never want to meet the native humans, because everyone will suffer the greed that Yahweh had done to all his moving creation of this contrasting planet. When I become the almighty, I will also reign here and make them and I will make everyone my servants".

Lucifer spread its huge wings and shaped itself into a large ball of burning red-hot fire and left the Earth flying through outer space. He ascended to Heaven, where he headed for his underworld, in order to continue the governability of his pernicious fever.

CHAPTER 7

OUTLINE OF A NEW PROJECT IN THE HEAVEN

Yahweh, faced with the unexpected occurrence of the Lucifer attack, on the third level, decided to take drastic measures. He, in addition to having allowed the angels Miguel and Gabriel to use the daggers for the Celestial Army, in their three corporations, also felt the need to reform Heaven. He visited the three levels, and, studying them, observed them to be places few inhospitable to heavenly angels. As for the third level, He realized that this place was suffering due to an unevenness, with a slightly deep cavity in it, where, above, the messenger angels and below, the executing angels of his orders.

Yahweh, therefore, was not pleased with the physical configurations of any of the levels created by Lucifer in his obsession project, which, perhaps, he could give him, as regards the attacks carried out by his evil spirits.

Due to his new architectural vision to make Heaven more secure, Yahweh, upon returning to the throne, outlined a new project to configure Heaven in all its perfection. When consolidating the draft of the project, He presented it to Emanuel saying: "I must change, what has to be changed, so that Heaven is a perfect work!"

As the three-tier project was conceived by Lucifer, who had succeeded in doing so due to the peculiar insistence on his wickedness, Yahweh united with the heavenly angels and, in an assembly, told them about his newly established project in the vacuum, which gave rise to the Universe and on it the planet Earth and the temporal life in it. He presented on a huge screen everything that existed in the Universe and, especially, on planet Earth. The Universe, He showed angel's space and all stars; the planets and other forms of matter in it. And on planet Earth, her mineral resources together with the products of the biosphere, which provided resources used for the life of her creatures from the animal, mineral and vegetable kingdoms and all their species.

The angels were delighted with the creation project of Yahweh and He made them understand that Heaven would soon be connected to the whole Universe, as if everything summed up in one, combined everything; the planet Earth would also be part of that connection, and all His creations and creatures would be part of this great project, as for the supernatural maintenance, which focused only through the faith to be worked among the higher beings endowed with intelligence. These superior beings were humans or "thinking inhabitants", whom Yahweh ordered to dominate all the kingdoms existing on the Terra plan.

After introducing the angels to the newly established project of the Universe, Yahweh also presented them with a draft of a new project in Heaven called "mutatis mutandis". Change by changing. In order to establish new orders to the kingdom, perpetuating it forever and ever.

In the "mutatis mutandis" project, the three levels would cease to exist and the entire space of Heaven of variable dimensions would become one around the pinnacle. Everything would be summed up in a large circle, as a flat surface limited by a curved line, with the sacred pinnacle in the center, and then positioned around the pinnacle the nine Choirs or Angelic Orders, divided into three hierarchies.

The first hierarchy would be formed by the seraphim; cherubs and thrones, the latter being reserved to welcome in itself the greatness of Yahweh and the transmission to the angels who would present to the lower choirs, the splendor of Divine Omnipotence. Yahweh would also make six more chariots of fire and deliver them to the seraphim angels, so that they could carry them according to the orders of the angel Af.

The second hierarchy called Dominations would be formed by the angels to direct the Plans of Eternal Wisdom, communicating the projects to the Angels of the Third Hierarchy, who, due to the creation of the Universe, would monitor the behavior of humans on planet Earth. In this hierarchy would be the ministers of Yahweh, formed by powers, the Conductors of the sacred order, who would be the transmitters of the power received by Yahweh, responsible for what should be done, taking special care of the "way" or "way" as sacred things must be done; the Virtues, to be composed of strong and virile angels whose tasks would compete in the mission of removing obstacles capable of interfering in the perfect fulfillment of Yahweh's orders.

The third hierarchy, where the angels who would carry out the orders of Yahweh would remain, being Principalities, guides of the divine messengers, the angels who will take the divine instructions and warnings, to the knowledge of the thinking inhabitants of the planet Earth that will be entrusted to him; the Archangels who would be the angels who know the deepest mysteries of Yahweh and who will be present before him and, finally, the Angels who will receive the orders of the upper choirs and execute them, being able to be close to the thinking inhabitants of the planet Earth, living with them and providing them with silent services, of immeasurable value to each of them.

The three corporations of the Celestial Army would be integrated into only one and would be in Heaven as a fortified wall to defend the pinnacle and the three hierarchies. The angels Miguel, Gabriel and the intercessor angel, Rafael, would be entrusted to the Celestial Army.

The "mutatis mutandis" project was happily elected by the angels and soon Yahweh carried it out with Emanuel. After the execution of the project "mutatis mutandis", Yahweh selected the angels from various hierarchies and took them over, according to their new functions.

The next step that would be taken by Yahweh, would be to create a single strong and shining light to manifest itself over all of Heaven, making it reveal all good and, as He knew that this light to be created would not be tolerated by Lucifer, postponed it.

Emanuel, with the help of the executing angels, made a huge golden plaque where he engraved in bold letters the following sentence: "Gloria in excelsis Deo, et pacem cum angelis caeli!" (Glory to God in the highest, peace, with the heavenly angels! And he affixed it above the throne of Yahweh).

When Lucifer returned to his underworld, he found Beelzebub sitting on a small throne next to his. Near the throne of Beelzebub there was a large, highly polished, metalized surface that reflected the image of anyone looking at it. Lucifer, seeing the mirror and his image reflected in it, did not like the idea. He therefore nurtured a certain painful and complex feeling in his own image. He demanded explanations about the mirror and Beelzebub replied: "Don't you see that his image is reflected in it? It serves to see our image, a significant mark that we represent in this place. Yahweh did not make us fully in his image and likeness, as he did to Emanuel, but you, Lucifer, can make those who follow your order in my image".

Lucifer feared being betrayed by Beelzebub and destroyed the mirror in pieces. Lucifer feared being betrayed by Beelzebub and destroyed the mirror in pieces. Beelzebub complained and he then, seeing him as vain, sprouted a pair of horns on Beelzebub's head, like that of the goat's species he had known on Earth, in one of the creations of Yahweh. Beelzebub scratched his head, felt the horns on his forehead, but tolerated the punishment, saying: "I hope that this gift given to me, by my lord, will make me the envy of all angels and that it will be, according to my desire, my image extended to the beings of its creation or transformation".

After feeling his head and confirming the horns on his forehead, Beelzebub tried to bring Lucifer up to date with his new plans. He suggested to Lucifer to create a new world, irreverent to Heaven, capable of expressing strength and value to attract the attention of all the angels of Yahweh. He suggested to Lucifer to transform that underworld into a "multi-world", an ostentatious, luxuriantly attractive place. Argument: "Therefore, for this, Lucifer, it will be necessary to take care of the images of everything and everyone who lives in this world, making them more perfect than those of Yahweh".

Beelzebub found the settings of the devils haunting and insisted that Lucifer should improve them, creating consistent and seductive images to them. He argued enthusiastically: "Beauty, Lucifer, is something seductive and behind it we will hide our intentions. See, I made a huge device to reflect our images. But when you noticed his image reflected in him, he caused a panic syndrome..."

Lucifer was clear that it was not the image of him reflected in the mirror that had caused the rage, but the fact that Beelzebub asked him to make his followers, his image. He postponed this and preferred to counter-argue Beelzebub's project about the due changes in his underworld. He, unlike the Beelzebub project, thought of constituting a world where there would be flames, a furnace of fire to destroy everything and all creatures of Yahweh. Beelzebub then corrected: "Behind a seductive scenario we will create our turkey and there we will condemn the captured angels..."

The turkey would be a foggy place and in that place Lucifer could reserve all the evils to be applied to the creatures of Yahweh. Lucifer let himself be convinced by the idea of Beelzebub and from then on he would take advantage of the new changes, creating scenarios and overlying things, which would serve as a trap for the whole creation of Yahweh. As Beelzebub knew all the angels of his second sphere, converted to Lucifer, he chose some to become leaders in the new scenario to be composed of him and Lucifer.

Lucifer, Beelzebub and some devotees, ex-cherubs chosen to lead the new world to be idealized, gathered at a huge table to discuss new projects for the world of Lucifer. The ex-leader of the cherubim, who was converted by Lucifer and helped him to persuade other angels, was invited to be part of the summit, being called Satan, a name that would imply "adversary of Yahweh". Lucifer gave him a new configuration, making him strong and fearless.

After the new world of Lucifer was idealized and designed by enigmatic drawings made by Beelzebub, Satan and other leaders, Lucifer, when studying it, did not accept it. Beelzebub and Satan wanted to know from him where the design error was. Lucifer said the project was perfect and just counter-argued in order to conquer the strength of his evil army to advance the attacks to be made in Heaven: "Until I dominate all of Heaven and the Universe and obtain my glory, I will not build my new kingdom".

Lucifer isolated himself on his throne and there he devised ways to achieve his main objective: the insurrection against Yahweh. The possessiveness of making Yahweh disappears and all creation clinging to Him rested in his mind. That end would be death, the definitive cessation of life or the existence of things that he did not like. He told Beelzebub and Satan that that little place in Heaven, to which they were accommodated, was temporary and when he officially became the omnipotent, he would complete the project, creating a new world, extending Heaven to the entire Universe and, mainly to planet Earth, where the entire creation of Yahweh would also dominate, including humans.

CHAPTER 8

THE MEN OF THE LANDS OF NODE

The seven angels transfigured into humans and abandoned by Lucifer, in the dense forest, were made wanderers over various regions of planet Earth. They walked through the dense forests, they rested by the lakes, they followed the cautious courses of the rivers and they went up and down mountains. As they walked, they admired everything that Yahweh had made to exist in every place on earth. Every now and then a terrible lizard would appear to threaten them dangerously, but they would defend themselves by hiding behind rock formations, mountains, hills and behind trees.

Once, on a dark, moonless night, as they descended a hill, the seven humanized angels heard strange cries. They tried to hide it, but the strange screams grew louder and closer to them. They thought it was the terrible lizards, but after the screaming stopped, they denoted some similar beings close to them. It was a flock of humans fleeing the attack of a terrible carnivorous lizard.

The seven humanized angels when perceiving the group of humans and without understanding why this group resembles their image, sought to observe them through the foliage of an advantageous bush. Thinking that the group of newly emerged humans there was also a group of angels, they rushed to join him. They did not succeed. The group of newly appeared humans in that place, on seeing the seven humanized angels, ran, fleeing aimlessly towards a low erosion of the valley, disappearing in a deep turkey.

The seven humanized angels, when they saw the group of humans dispersing towards the deep turkey of the valley, conferences were given on what they saw and when their similarities to that of men were shown. They were happy to find themselves not being alone on Earth. After that event, they slept on the lawn, under a tall tree and at dawn they felt something empty in the bodies and the strange need to fill them with something. Their stomachs, depending on the plague of Lucifer, awoke to greed. They saw some trees of the genus malus, of the rosaceous family and the branches of these trees hanging from round and red fruits. They harvested them and, for the first time, tasted something from a certain tree on Earth. These fruits they called apple, because they were soft and fragrant and gave a feeling of relief to the strange pain they felt in the stomach. In this way, Lucifer's plague of making the seven humanized angels feel the same needs of natural humans on Earth was fulfilled: hunger. This, however, implied greed for humans, as to the desire to eat and drink until they were fully satisfied. The desire to eat and drink indicated to the seven angels a warning of control, since, according to them, any immoderate desire would not be seen as a good, in the eyes of Yahweh.

The seven human angels, after taking possession of Lucifer's punishment, on greed, began to walk the Earth through the places where rivers and fruit plants existed due to the need to quench thirst and hunger.

Again, while the seven angels were resting by the lake, after a large meal, two huge lizards appeared and tried to catch them. They were running to get rid of the monsters, when, suddenly, another group of native humans appeared, with huge spears in their hands and helped them to defend themselves against the huge reptiles.

After the native humans defended the seven humanized angels from the terrible lizards, they took them in and brought them to them, making them know a safe and habitable place. The seven humanized angels accepted the invitation of the native humans and, as they went on, they arrived at a wonderful place, where all kinds of abundance flowed. The place was a plain formed by the elongated depression of a river and in it there was a field with all kinds of abundant vegetation where they removed their food, collecting fruits, grains and roots which they ate raw.

The seven humanized angels observed the way of life of the

humans of the tribe and admired the instruments used by them in carrying out their work, which consisted of making instruments, pulling out roots and defending themselves against dangerous lizards. As for the instruments, men made hand axes, arrowheads and small spears with stones, animal bones and branches or dry wood, hitting them on the stones until they were shaped to cut, scrape or drill, whatever they needed. They also observed that most humans were constantly moving from place to place in search of food, or sometimes due to geographic factors, cold, snow, rain, heat, etc. With the appearance of terrible lizards, most of them were preserved in safe places, choosing valleys of fertile soils of varying vegetation. The fact that they feed on fruits, grains and roots, they hunt and kill only a few species of animals to remove their hair and / or hides, which, after tanning them in the sun and beating them, served as clothing to the body.

The tribe known to the seven humanized angels had acquired a new shape to the clothing of the body, since they, without a doubt, sharpened the bones of animals, pierced the leather and made use of tendons, dried guts or strips of leather as threads and sewed their own clothes. They were also concerned with the division of tasks, women took care of the young and, with them, were responsible for the collection of fruits and roots; men hunted, fished and defended the territory of their tribes.

The seven humanized angels realized that, in that valley, men, women and their respective offspring lived in communion, having as concern, only the unforeseen attacks of the terrible lizards.

Due to the fact that the seven humanized angels are spiritually different, the native humans admired them and, for this reason, made them live in their tribe, where, there, they were inserted to the same degree of kinship.

The tribe that welcomed the seven humanized angels was divided into three clans or family groups, from the same ethnic group who shared the same language and customs. In this tribe, each clan referred to a generation and, therefore, there was a degree of affiliation in the direct line, with the third lineage. The seven humanized angels came to live together in this great tribe and, over time, they harmoniously learned to deal with the tasks of men and also, making use of secular insights, helped them to perfect techniques when doing things and to introduce new words in their lexicon.

The tribesmen, due to the positive appreciations of the seven humanized angels, soon maintained a collective organization and helped each other, mutually, always in search of new perspectives to ease the hard tasks imposed on them, on Earth, which were summarized in the survival.

After times and many times of living together on planet Earth, the seven humanized angels became totally involved in the geographical context in which they lived and, as a way of acquiring their identities, they adopted Earth as the "great mother" (the word mother, according to them, it would be related to the matrix, as that from which other things originate) and, when they joined it, they chose proper names from the things that existed in it to self-determine: bird, river, seed, universe, sea; mineral and energy. It was up to the angel Ave to teach humans about the specimen of birds. He would be in charge of studying birds, classifying them, according to their species and giving names, according to their characteristics; it would be up to the angel Rio to study and teach about rivers, tributaries and, finally, about the entire natural course of fresh water, classifying and naming them according to geographical and route accidents; it would be up to the angel seed to teach about the structures of fruits and their importance of harvesting seeds from them, preserving, planting and also transporting them to other regions as an embryo to give rise to new plants, according to their species; to the angel Universe, that of conjecturing to humans about space - stars, planets and other forms of matter existing in it, valuing the entire creation of Yahweh; the angel Mar would have to teach men about the part of the surface of the planet Earth that was formed by water and, possibly, about all the species that exist on it. The

Mineral angel would be responsible for teaching about the realm of non-organic things and their possible combinations, classifying and naming them, according to their characteristics in the parts of the earth's crust. To the angel Energy the task of teaching about the potential capacity of men to carry out their work, transforming their potential into an activity and to defend themselves from the natural phenomena affected on Earth, due to the potential and expansion of the Universe.

After the seven humanized angels chose their respective names, according to each task they were destined to teach to the thinking inhabitants of the Earth, they also taught the designation of proper names for them, their women and, respectively, their offspring who were born of the blessed mother womb of his women. The native men of the tribe adhered to the idea of the seven angels and started to use their own names for themselves, their women and their sons and daughters. To the older couple and parent of all clans of the tribe, the children presented them with the following names: Node, the parent and Avena, the parent or mother. After that the great tribe of the three clans came to be called "lands of Node", with the Earth being divided into territories or delimited areas under the possession of the sons of Node and Avena, it started to have common characteristics, becoming its own only when referring to the Planet of the solar system inhabited by man.

After getting used to the rituals of proper names, the men of lands of Node started to name geographical places, biology, botany, zoology and also the usual and unclean things.

The tribe of the lands of Node, welcoming the seven humanized angels, reached the fourth generation of their descendants and chiefs, with the intention of creating bonds with the seven humanized angels, chose seven virgin women and gave them as gifts to them whose purpose would be so that these virgin women could conceive children of the seven humanized angels to constitute degrees of kinship and a faithful lineage to the clans.

The seven humanized angels joined the virgin women and

formed families, the offspring, they called them children, observing the fact that they pass through several phases until they become men or women capable of solving problems. They conceived strong descendants and leaders with authorities and charismas to command other clans to which they emerged.

The seven humanized angels unified the tribe of the Lands of Node and managed them respecting all divine creation, contributing to their future generations to new evolutions.

When a lightning bolt broke at the top of a mountain announcing stormy storms, the thinking inhabitants of the land feared this phenomenon and retreated to safe places, now in caves or inside their fragile huts. After this phenomenon, they saw and reported on some animals and / or also humans who died near the trees affected and set on fire by lightning. Faced with this fact common to human beings everywhere on planet Earth, the angel Energy began to study the entire course of storms and, when there was a serious phenomenon of lightning hitting some part of the earth, close to his tribe, he, courageously, he left his hut to observe the phenomenon. Initially, he thought it was a manifestation of Yahweh on Planet Earth, but as this phenomenon often caused things to die and destroy some things in nature, this action could not be Yahweh's. Then he raised another possibility that a lightning bolt, derived from storms and lightning, was a way for the Lord to warn all the creatures of the earth about the rain, making them take shelter in safe places to defend themselves from the action of nature. The angel Seed made the angel Energy understand that rain is important to water the plants and make the seeds spread by the wind, which fell in lands far from the rivers; he was also responsible for teaching children some important tasks, making it easy for them to understand the importance of life and things on Earth; the angel Rio argued about the importance of rain to supply the tributaries, whose mission would be to sustain the sea with the fallen waters in various parts of the Earth.

If Brother Energy was interested in observing the phenomena

of lightning, he once, after a storm, ran over the forest and when he saw the fire burning a tree, he collected it and took it to the tribe. There, he kept the fire burning in the shape of a bonfire and gave the larger chicks the task of keeping it always lit, feeding the fire with sticks and wooden logs. From this important event, the tribes of the seven humanized angels began to manipulate fire both in domestic actions - roasting meat and cooking vegetables -, as well as to protect themselves from the cold and the attacks of ferocious animals.

Over time, fire has become the main transformative agent of new inventions for more civilized tribes. The seven humanized angels helped their tribe to evolve by teaching its members to domesticate animals, to harvest the fruits at the right time, to choose the seeds of the fruits and to plant them in fertile lands, to preserve the affluent and all nature and to observe the greatness of Universe, especially at night, when Heaven was enchanted with its stars. All of this served to encourage men from any part of the planet Earth.

The seven humanized angels, drawing on their experiences of heavenly spirits, also taught their children and made them also teach their neighbors about the things of heaven and the importance of them knowing Yahweh and giving Him worship and praise services. The Universe and the Earth and everything and all men and women and children and animals and things, which existed in them, served them to demonstrate the greatness of Yahweh. They never told the stories about them, about how they were put on Earth to avoid mentioning Lucifer's name and his terrible features due to the envy and ambition of Yahweh's power. They were responsible for teaching only the good to serve the good. They thought of Lucifer and reflected among themselves, on the sly: "Ab esse ad posse valet consequentia". (There is strength in the relationship between the event and the possibility of it happening). It would be better, therefore, never to mention the name of the angel or demon who had become the enemy of the Creator.

There were other tribes distant from the region where the

inhabitants of the tribe of the lands of Node lived, however, the most evolved was that of Node, whose generation came to the fifth and, each of these generations changed their configuration as the years went on.

CHAPTER 9

BEELZEBUB AND SATAN IN THE UNIVERSE

Time and time later, Lucifer took Beelzebub and Satan to visit the Universe and, especially, the planet Earth. The three traveled through the cosmos and were amazed by the organized and harmonious ensemble: space and all the stars, planets and other forms of matter in it. When Beelzebub and Satan arrived on planet Earth and stepped on the solid part of its surface, they were even more dazzled by everything that Lucifer presented them on this planet: plants, rivers, lakes, waterfalls, sea, animals, and all their species and other species of animate and inanimate beings.

Lucifer was repairing the feelings of Beelzebub and Satan during that trip. He feared that the whole balance of those things created by Yahweh would make them convert again to their old posts in Heaven. He knew that whoever traveled under the ethereal and was able to feel the sublimity and supremacy of all things constituted in him, would end up destitute themselves. if from evil. Lucifer feared this would happen to his two main leaders. Then he, maliciously, began to criticize the things Yahweh instituted on Earth, telling them that he would do it otherwise.

At the moment when Lucifer criticized the things instituted on planet Earth, three terrible lizards suddenly appeared in the place where they were. Beelzebub and Satan looked at each other and began to criticize the giant, devastating animals. Satan commented: "Everything I've seen so far contains all the Creator's harmony and authenticity, but these huge, disproportionate animals have nothing to do with this world ..." Beelzebub also seriously commented: "It's true, Satan, I believe that Yahweh has overblown a little, look at the difference between these animals and the others presented to us, by

Lucifer... ”

Lucifer fixed his eyes on a passing herd of reptiles, scratched his head a little embarrassed and replied: “And they still say that the execution of the owner of things is perfect! Aim for those animals! See how terrible they are! ” Satan concluded it: “The reason for an extravagant creation like that of these terrible lizards should be viable explanations. We have to agree and accept that everything done by Yahweh is perfect! ”

Lucifer did not like the ending of Satan and, silently, transported them to the top of a hill, in a desert and arid place. Upon reaching this hill, he made the two companions observe the whole region and bluffed sarcastically: “Look at another imperfection of that Creator, where he saw such an ugly place, it seems that he forgot to create plants, animals and things in these parts ... Not even humans live in it ... ”

Beelzebub wanted to know from Lucifer what the humans were or was just mentioned. Lucifer replied: “They are superior beings on earth, endowed with insight and penetrated with spirit, just as Yahweh did the heavenly angels, there are also angels on earth; but they are different, flowed through an aggregate body of particles that make up mass. Yahweh made them and charged them with taking care of everything that exists on this arid and harsh planet...”

Satan showed interest in meeting humans: "And why haven't we seen him on this Planet"?

Lucifer thought quickly and replied: "Why do surprises remain at the end of our journey ..."

Satan and Beelzebub were silent and then, Lucifer looked at the Earth's landscapes, looked up at the Universe and spoke loudly, in order for his voice to resonate everywhere on Earth: “Here I will make one of my addresses and command the entire Universe and the whole Earth and everything in it!”

When Lucifer declared this, the mountain, which, he did not know was consecrated to Yahweh, began to tremble and the burning salsa, like gas, to catch fire, expelled a salty mud and launched itself towards him, Satan and Beelzebub. They withdrew quickly from the mount and landed on a flat surface of the Earth.

Lucifer thought that the phenomenon was an authorship of his power, but Satan made him realize that the mountain would be like the pinnacle of Yahweh, "a place guarded by Him, for Him alone".

Satan's assumption about the mountain as a pinnacle of Yahweh made Lucifer furious and, as his next step would be to bring them to the attention of humans, he took Beelzebub and Satan to a place where Yahweh had created, with a favorable climate, to all species of animals existing on planet Earth. This place contained about 30 million square kilometers, covering 20.3% of the total land area of the planet. Upon reaching this place, Lucifer introduced them to a bunch of ugly, grotesque and misshapen individuals and all their species. These animals would jump from branches on tree branches, make noise and scare the animals, sometimes even ride on them. These animals were primates, or monkeys, characterized by humans for having more or less straight snouts and nostrils directed downwards, fingers with fingernails, thumbs and the largest opposable toes and teeth with two premolars. Lucifer made them watch the monkeys, saying: "They are the angels of the earth whom Yahweh gave insight to take care of and everything in it..."

Beelzebub and Satan found the humans funny and burst out laughing. Beelzebub commented: "Strange, they have the perfection of heavenly angels, but their body structures are versatile. See, notice how many skills they have to deal with plants and animals..."

Lucifer heard some rumors of humans over there and quickly took off in a shallow, accurate flight. He left Beelzebub and Satan alone, watching the monkeys, and landed quietly in a dense forest, where there was a plateau and five human clans lived in it. The families of the five tribes were gathered around a brazier roasting some game to feed themselves.

Lucifer fearing that the tribes were discovered by the two friends, logically thought of transforming the members of the three tribes into an appearance that approached the monkeys. He did not hesitate and immediately tried to turn all the inhabitants of the five tribes into dark skins, saying: "After eating this slaughtered and burning animal in embers, I will make them as black as night and by absorbing all luminous radiations, they will make, their skins missing color. This will extend to all your descendants forever. " Lucifer snuck out of there. He rejoined his companions again, arguing: "I left in search of something new that I could introduce them to, but I found nothing..."

The inhabitants of the five tribes, to whom Lucifer manifested his character, after being satisfied with the game roasted in coals, lost their body hair and transmuted to black. They, in their primary conceptions, raised hypotheses thinking that it was the type of game and / or the way it was roasted and also the charcoal, because they were all the color of the brand. Some, desperate, screamed and curled up in the grass; others threw themselves into a nearby stream to wash their bodies and get rid of black pigmentation. The commotion of the inhabitants of the three tribes was like a battle cry and this caught the attention of Beelzebub and Satan. Lucifer pretended to hear nothing and tried to drag the two friends to other places on Earth, but they, curious, made a quick sweep and spotted the inhabitants of the five tribes who were afflicted with the punishment merit.

Lucifer flew towards the two friends and forbade them to approach the inhabitants of the tribes, saying that they were also humans created by Yahweh to the same extent as those who jumped on the tree branches. They obeyed Lucifer and continued their tour elsewhere on planet Earth.

Lucifer, in his intense evil, did not rectify his transformation made to the inhabitants of the five tribes, departing, later on, with his companions for his underworld. He again left another mark on planet Earth of his unfortunate transformation and, as a result, he raised these five tribes to the lineage of the black ethnicity, this ethnic group being healthier and more likely to reproduce than individuals from the tribes of clear skins.

CHAPTER 10

THE NODE VILLAGE

Years and years passed in the Universe and the terrible giant animals, both aquatic and terrestrial, adapted to it. The terrible lizards had scaly and waterproof skins and they laid eggs with harsh shells, facilitating the proliferation of their species, both herbivorous and carnivorous. They moved quickly through various places on Earth in search of food and when they met with predatory enemies, they fled quickly.

Humans, known in some early tribes as men and women, had no peace due to the attacks of the terrible lizards. Some tribes tried to domesticate them, but they did not realize it due to the space and uncontrollable food.

In search of safe places, genuine tribes began to unite with other ethnicities, varying lineages, degrees of culture, religion, language and behavior.

The tribe of the lands of Node, which comprised the seven humanized angels, reached the sixth generation. There, all the inhabitants, under the constant guidance of the seven humanized angels, converted their intrinsic values to religion centered on Yahweh's belief in the creation of the world and everything that existed in it, with respect and reverence for sacred things, from food, actions taken, days lived and nature and the entire Universe.

With the passing of the moons, the seven humanized angels, seeing that it was not enough just to speak of Yahweh to men, decided to establish a sacred temple in the lands of Node where they would meet every seven days with men in the same place to teach them how to render obeisance's to Yahweh.

After many studies, the Universe angel recommended the six humanized angels to choose a high mountain, where they would approach the Sun and the Moon and be able to aim at nature in all its perfection. The six humanized angels accepted the idea of the universe angel and when choosing a hill, they instituted the sacred temple in it, making it open to the sky, resplendent to all creation of Yahweh.

The seven humanized angels called the mountain "Heaven", due to its altitude and, every seven days - representation linked to them, as they were seven angels from Heaven - they and the men of the tribe of the lands of Node climbed the mountain and there they bowed to Yahweh, thanking him for all the creatures on planet Earth and asking for thanks for the perpetuation of all of them.

From the extreme dedications to Yahweh made every seven days in the "Temple of Heaven", the seven humanized angels made the trust in Yahweh, by humans, become an important belief among future generations. This belief based on the obeisance's to Yahweh made men and their coming generations to feel comfortable and useful for the Earth, both to unify work; as to respect for universal creation and solidarity between them and adjacent or distant tribes.

The confidence and comfort found by the humans of the tribes of the lands of Node, in the "Temple of Heaven", gradually raised other men from neighboring and distant tribes, serving to make them understand the meaning of life, knowing their origins and the reason for being in the world.

When witnessing the services given to Yahweh, in the "Temple of Heaven", men understood the meaning of life, summarizing it, basically in four important aspects: respect for Yahweh, above all else; the care of the existence of everything that Yahweh created on Earth, respecting, protecting and giving perpetuation to all species; respect for others, consisting of living in peace with families, with all other tribes and, finally, of showing solidarity in a reciprocal way or communion.

The curiosity about the sacred services held in the "Temple of Heaven" brought men from various places and these, upon meeting the tribe of the Lands of Node and listening to the preaching of the seven humanized angels, set up camps near it and ended up taking place there. In this way, in a short time the tribe of the Node lands took on great importance in relation to the surrounding areas and, where there was only one tribe, it began to be characterized in a small village called "Node Village".

In Village of Node, everyone learned the secrets of Divine Creation and everyone worked mutually, always perfecting their arts and crafts, important impulses to make them the first inhabitants of planet Earth to wear clothes made of interwoven fibers, of vegetable origin, which, although they were rustic, they were much lighter and more comfortable than those made of fur. Like the services of the "Sacred Temple", this new way of dressing the body, also attracted the attention of humans from other tribes who sought them out to learn the art of how to make them and ended up migrating to Node Village, with their clans.

The Village of Node became an important pole of migration for humans who lived scattered in various parts of the Earth, either as nomads or fixed, and who needed security and comfort for their tribal societies. All were welcomed into the village, acquiring land for the construction of their homes and crops necessary for subsistence.

The seven humanized angels witnessing the increasing number of men in knowing and converting to the beliefs of Yahweh, in addition to doing the services in the "Temple of Heaven", also started to do them in the center of the village, whose celebration took place in around a huge bonfire called "Yahweh's alibi", alluding to the affirmation of the presence of Yahweh in different places on planet Earth, including that place, where all the inhabitants of the village and newcomers gathered in communion with the sacred.

The "Yahweh's alibi" bonfire was awakened during the night in the form of a vigil, every three days after the services in the "Temple of Heaven", giving men, women and their respective children the opportunity to participate collectively. The purpose of this fiery ceremony was to raise Yahweh to the liberation of their souls. This form of consecration of the soul was also a way of raising awareness and affirming to humans the presence of Yahweh among them, in that place and or in any other place to which He was acclaimed.

The "Yahweh's alibi" campfire has become an archetype to other neighboring tribes and, over time, has extended to other distant ones, which sometimes received, in an honorable way, the visits of the seven humanized angels and also of their descendants.

One day, Lucifer, disguised as a human, returned to planet Earth to observe his features on it. He, thinking that the terrible lizards had damaged everything on Earth, was very sad. The planet Earth was intact, because all living beings had enough food and each species adapted to a region consolidated to their needs.

He visited some tribes and found men, women and children working harmoniously, both in the fields and in household chores. On some nights he also witnessed, around great bonfires of crackling flames, some clans worshiping Yahweh, thanking him for all his creation on Earth. He was furious and remembered the seven humanized angels abandoned there, by him. He thought: "The seven angels transformed into humans, would certainly be responsible for spreading the power and virtues of Yahweh, over the whole Earth".

Lucifer searched all regions of planet Earth where cults predominated and, in a place, where a lot of houses were lined up in straight lines and others in winding lines, he discovered the Village of Node. Pretending to be an alien, coming from a region far from somewhere on that planet, he surveyed some residents of Node Village and discovered that the seven humanized angels were practically the ones who managed it. Someone took him to the presence of the angel Universe and this when he received Lucifer, in his complete disguise, made him reach the other six humanized angels. The seven humanized angels received him as he received all the pilgrims who arrived there, offering him the best in their homes.

Lucifer, concealing admirations for the village and the services given to Yahweh, wanted to know about the ordinary activities of the seven humanized angels. The angels Energy and Seed invited him for a walk through the village of Node and, during the route, they told him about his experiences and why that place attracted so many souls, who, in a complete way, migrated there. Lucifer became interested in the "Temple of Heaven" and the bonfires called "Yahweh's alibi" which were lit in communion with the sacred.

Lucifer, taking advantage of the kindness, patience and generosity of the seven humanized angels, stayed for a few days in the house of the angel Universe whose family was always prepared as a good host for newcomers to the village. He, like everyone who arrived there, showed interest in participating in the service at the "Temple of Heaven". Later, he joined the seven humanized angels and all the men in the village of Node to climb the hill with them and participate in the worship of Yahweh. He participated and pretended to be amazed at the service. He also waited for three days, after the worship of the Holy Temple, to participate in the "Yahweh's alibi" ceremony. As for this ceremony, he devised an evil plan which implied to expel the seven humanized angels from the planet Earth.

When the third day that the night of vigil happened, in the village of Node, men, women and their respective children came together during the afternoon to collect firewood and start the big fire. At night, the seven humanized angels approached the great bonfire, blessed it and set it on fire, dedicating with perseverance some important rituals of the ceremony to Yahweh. While the seven angels were performing the blessed rituals of the sacred ceremony, Lucifer looked at the crackling fire, waiting for the right moment to put his evil plan into practice.

At the end of the ceremony and, before the fire consumed the wood and the high flames ceased, Lucifer approached the seven humanized angels and asked them: "Do they constitute copies of your copies here, do they not"? The angel Energy took the lead of the other six humanized angels and replied: "Yes, our copies are called family, since we started to belong to Earth; we give it as a contribution to our descendants".

Lucifer, without showing any surprise, observing the lack of malice of the angel Energy, took advantage of this to continue to probe the humanized angels: "You made all the tribes know about the power and virtues of Yahweh on planet Earth, no made"? The angel Universe replied, humbly: "We did it, because just as He created Heaven and the Universe and everything in them, we are also the results of His creatures..."

Lucifer got rid of the image of a man, who made him pass for an alien and transformed himself into a beautiful angel, saying: "Like you, I am also a creature of Yahweh and I inhabit Heaven in all its glory".

The transformation of Lucifer into an angel from heaven surprised all the men, women and children who were present there. Everyone marveled at the figure of the beautiful angel. The seven angels looked at Lucifer disguised as an angel and thought about the possibility that he was an envoy of Yahweh to observe the planet Earth and evaluate the services rendered to Him.

The angel Seed, full of splendor and charm, stood in front of the false angel and spoke proudly: "We were heavenly angels and we were transfigured into humans and abandoned here on Earth by an angel much loved by Yahweh and who became wicked. Earth, this great mother welcomed us, and, as we are creatures of Yahweh, both in Heaven and on Earth, we make living seeds to bring forth knowledge about His power and glory to all living beings endowed with intelligence ".

Lucifer, hearing the spontaneous and instantaneous outburst of the angel Seed, gnashed his teeth secretly, looked at the fire, for everyone present and said to the seven angels: "Yahweh said it is time for you to return to Heaven and give thanks to Him on his eternal throne".

The seven humanized angels knelt and replied to the false

angel in Heaven: "Let the will of our Yahweh be done!" They cheered Yahweh, telling everyone about the importance of the "Yahweh's alibi" ceremony, because he was present there, through an angel sent by Him. Everyone looked at the false angel from Heaven and also fell on their knees praising cries to Yahweh.

The false angel of Heaven made the seven humanized angels and everyone got up, and, using all their evil, made the fire spew horrible flames to the point of making everyone frighten and turn away from it. Then, using a centrifugal force, he hurled the seven humanized angels to the center of the fire. The seven humanized angels, when thrown to the center of the fire, lost the characteristics of humans and became again angels with all the celestial apparatuses, as they had arrived at the planet Earth. Everyone there, away from the fire, though scared, screamed in amazement as they watched the transfigurations of the seven angels. The seven angels were suspended by the fire, held hands in a circle and said goodbye to everyone in the village of Node, saying in leather: "Be faithful to Yahweh, because it is from Him that all the resources necessary for life come". They, together with the smoke, flew through space until they disappeared from the eyes of the village crowd. The show impressed everyone. "Alia jacta est!" (Luck was cast!).

Lucifer, without understanding what had happened, spread his huge wings and disappeared from there, returning towards his kingdom. There, he conspired, together with Satan and Beelzebub, consistent ideas in order to dominate humanity.

The event of the night when the seven humanized angels were thrown at the "Yahweh's alibi" fig tree strengthened the faith of all the inhabitants of Node Village. All men, women and their children served as witnesses and began to propagate, wherever they went, the noble event in the village of Node, proposing faith in the glory of Yahweh. The place where the fire was erected for the "Yahweh's alibi" ceremonies became a sacred field, and it did not take long to become a space for a tent made of rustic fabric and with beautiful prints of the seven humanized angels. . This tent built with Yahweh, with the pattern of the seven humanized angels, served as an archetype to so many others built in various regions of the Earth, helping men to establish new villages and to grant good and peace among them.

The men, living in villages, strengthened their ideas based on the exchange of experiences and soon started to work collectively, mainly in hunting and fishing. The women's tasks consisted of ensuring the well-being of the villages, taking care of their children and subsistence agriculture. They emerged from the first leisure activities and, with the knowledge of fire, as a transforming agent, they created the art and technique of making baked clay objects, ceramics, which, over time, served as a commercialization among them, being, initially, a trade based on product exchanges, then based on currencies, represented by colored seeds. Since most of the villages appeared close to the rivers, men invented the canoe made of tree trunk excavated by fire and moved by oar, a small and very useful vessel as a means of transport, capable of getting them from one village to another. another, now in search of resources, in exchange for new experiences, now to witness the worship of Yahweh in the "Temple of Heaven" and the bonfire of the "Yahweh's alibi" ceremony, subsisted thanks to the generations of the seven humanized angels and by all inhabitants of Node Village.

Since the time when the seven humanized angels were thrown on the fire and ascended in the form of angels to Heaven, the funerals of the faithful adherents to the tents built up to Yahweh have gained a new funeral garment. Everyone who died had their bodies burned at the stake, which were lit in the churchyard of the sacred tents. From then on the established belief would be that the flame, as a material and visible part of the fire, would take the dead to Heaven, transforming them into angels so that they would live together forever with Yahweh and the seven angels. The bodies of the dead were turned into ashes and this was denoted as if they were transported to Heaven. If by chance some corpse did not become reduced to ashes, they would take the toasted remains and hand them over to the families. These placed the toasted remains in a ceramic vase - a mortuary urn - and buried them in a place considered sacred. They added to the new religious belief that if the body of the deceased was not reduced to ashes, it would be because he had not been able to enter Heaven.

Therefore, if he buried the parts not completely burned, he would be reborn from the earth, he would live again and, after his other death, and he would be able to become an angel in Heaven. This happened rarely, because the firewood was well calculated for the construction of the cremation fires, ensuring, through them, the reduction of bodies in ashes.

CHAPTER 11

THE THREE CHEATING ARCHANGELS

The seven humanized angels, after being thrown into the fire, got rid of Lucifer and flew to Heaven. Upon reaching Heaven, they came across the phrase posted by Miguel "Gloria in excelsis Deo, et pacem cum angelis caeli!" (Glory to God in the highest, peace, with the angels of heaven!). They were dazzled by the new change in the sacred kingdom. The three levels no longer existed and the entire space of Heaven of variable dimensions became one around the pinnacle, summing up in a large circle. As they belonged to the third level of messenger angels and executors of the orders of Yahweh, they would occupy the third circle. They flew into that circle and when they landed there the sky shuddered with joy and their bodies took on the outline of an aura of a spiritually high nature, being represented by an incandescent light. All the angels, archangels, cherubs and seraphim, when they saw the seven angels with the bodies outlined by the divine aura, knelt in their due circles. The seven humanized angels did not understand what was happening and also knelt at their proper posts. The seraphim angels flew towards them and, with fire chariots, they transported them comfortably to the center of the pinnacle, taking them to the throne of Yahweh.

The seven humanized angels, upon being placed before the throne, knelt and worshiped Yahweh, who made them rise, saying: "You bring the spiritually high nature aura in your complexions and this demonstrates to all of us that you have gone through a great trajectory to return to Heaven again. You will receive all the beatitudes that the elect in heaven enjoy, because you bring the sign of the resurrection, the return to life after death".

In saying this Yahweh blessed the seven angels, who, from humanized, became resurrected and invited them to tell him about their trajectories on planet Earth. The seven resurrected angels told Yahweh, through confession, about everything that happened to them on planet Earth.

The fact that the seven angels remain faithful to Yahweh, in exile to Earth and teach humans their eternal values through the "Temple of Heaven" and the fire of the "Yahweh's alibi" ceremony, the Creator saw the possibility of returning to life after death and this He would apply to men converted to Him, through purgation, making them eternal angels in Heaven. Yahweh, in thinking of this possibility, gave the seven resurrected angels the task of caring for the souls of humans, making them capable of reach Heaven, after death, through the process of release. He created a new sphere around the pinnacle, calling it "Aura sanctorum animae". (Aura of the sacred soul). He entrusted the seven resurrected angels to the custody of humanity, giving them the degree of power to examine men closely, helping them to get rid of evils. Yahweh told them: "Lucifer discovered the planet Earth and is looking for a perfect terrain to plant the chaff of doom; therefore, you, my guardian angels, will have the tough task of protecting humanity by watching over it. If the power of evil invests powerfully on Earth, drawing unguarded men to you, making you lose the sense of good and evil and the belief that everything will be allowed, you will have the arduous task of converting them back to me. "

The seven resurrected angels came to be designated as guardian angels and their tasks were reduced to watching over the spiritual and corporal life of men, diverting them from temporal and spiritual dangers, and also interceding for them in their multiple needs. Yahweh's infinite wisdom had given them free access to planet Earth, enabling them to fulfill their missions, invisibly. They would surely serve all of humanity, preventing it from falling into the tricks of Lucifer and his evil army.

After Yahweh created the new circle attributed to "Aura of the sacred soul", located between the third hierarchy and the fort - the Celestial Army -, and when he handed it over to the seven resurrected angels (or guardian angels), he gave them to a compendium of rules of procedure to be studied and applied to humanity, depending on material life, entitled "Arte coniunctum tangibile lucra". (Closely linked to tangible assets). In this compendium there were seven important items on the main virtues for understanding material life on the plumb of spiritual life, considered correct and desirable to Yahweh. It implied readings on moral qualities, such as temperance, modesty, generosity, justice, strength and prudence, capable of improving men by making them stable, as to the usual perfections of human intelligence and will, regulating human beings. their actions in order to lead them to a life attuned to the greatness of Heaven and the Universe. These virtues would only be applied to humanity after Yahweh returned to the Universe and, exclusively, to the planet Earth to fulfill the promise made through the affiliation of the twenty-first generation of the prototype couple of human.

In heaven there were three archangels Sabah, Dom and Egerius. They also longed to be part of the newly created circle called "Aura of the sacred soul". Yahweh made these three archangels understand that the new instituted circle belonged to the seven guardian angels, because they went through the resurrection process. This would imply the power of them not only to belong to Heaven, but also to the Universe. They were eternally exempt from all evils that any angel from Heaven could come to suffer.

The three archangels met secretly and confabulated with each other against everything and everyone in heaven. They did not accept the autonomy of the seven guardian angels, conceived by Yahweh; even more so that angels have the power to go to Earth and become intercessors of the thinking creatures that exist there. Although Sabah, Dom and Egerius did not know the Universe, they thought it was a place superior to Heaven and, as for the thinking inhabitants of Earth, or humans, they believed as beings superior to all the heavenly angels and that, perhaps, Yahweh applied special powers to them. The word power implied Sabah, Dom and Egerius the dominion over everything that existed in Heaven and in the Universe and, therefore, they thought that the power should be for all the heavenly angels, mainly the angels of higher hierarchies.

By holding several meetings and conferences on the sly and persisting in the discussion of power as a right of angels and their respective hierarchies, the three archangels Sabah, Dom and Egerius disseminated new ideas raised against Yahweh in some circles of Heaven. angels who adhered to their speeches tried to convince other angels to join the insurrection movement against the Creator. The campaign of Sabah, Dom and Egerius, was gradually gaining strength, including among supporters from the Celestial Army. Everything was kept secret and everyone was preparing to implode a great rebellion in Heaven at any moment. Archangel Sabah, responsible for reporting to Yahweh about everything that happened in Heaven, reinforced the secret, making him believe that everything was about perfect order.

Archangels, as well as seraphim, had the right to come and go everywhere in Heaven, in order to visit the circles, according to each order established by Yahweh. Archangel Sabah being one of the main reporting angels of Yahweh, Archangel Dom gave him the idea of visiting the circle of the "Aura of the sacred soul" to investigate the mission of the seven resurrected angels. Sabah accepted Dom's idea and asked one of the seraphim to take him, in the fire chariot, to the room of the seven resurrected angels. Sabah, upon reaching the desired circle, was received with joy by the seven resurrected angels. These, knowing that Sabah was an important Yahweh reporter, trusted to report to him about their future missions on planet Earth and the important studies they were doing around the booklet or compendium of rules of procedure to be applied to humanity. Sabah found it very interesting and, after returning to his circle, he told the archangels Dom and Egerius about the accounts given to him by the seven resurrected angels. The three archangels observed and raised the seven virtues to be applied to humans on Earth and were surprised to learn that only those who, rightly fulfilling them, had the right to eternalize themselves in Heaven, after the process of death. They raised hypotheses about this information and came to think that humans, by clearing themselves, could acquire powers in Heaven, becoming more important than they, in the eyes of the Creator. This hypothesis left the three archangels jealous, to the point of becoming bitter and professing heavily against Yahweh.

Archangel Egerius let himself be embarrassed by the seven virtues to be applied to humans on Earth and, without measuring consequences, sought out some angels from the Celestial Army who had adhered to his, Sabah's and Dom's plans, to help him out. from Heaven. As soon as he got help, he fled Heaven's hierarchies and flew quickly to Lucifer's underworld. There, he intended to confer with Lucifer a possible and terrible rebellion against Yahweh.

Upon reaching Lucifer's underworld, Egerius came across the huge network of lozenges that surrounded Lucifer's entire space and, in an attempt to break through it, enter unexpectedly, ended up being stuck to it. Lucifer's devils discovered him trapped in the diamond net and captured him, bringing him to the attention of Lucifer.

When Egerius was placed before the throne of Lucifer, he was questioned by him, Beelzebub and Satan. He foolishly told Lucifer and the two cronies about his desire and that of the other two archangels, Sabah and Dom, about the possible insurrection against Yahweh. Lucifer, thinking it was a plan against him, set up by the archangel Egerius at the behest of Yahweh, gave orders to the devils to take him to them and keep him in prison until a second order. Egerius was carried by the devils and tossed among them, and then his feet, hands and wings were chained. He stayed there for a long, long time, feeling uncomfortable and regretting having made such a drastic decision, the consequence of which was directed at him.

Times and times later, when Egerius was questioned again by Lucifer, when he wanted to get rid of that place, he told him about everything he knew about the seven resurrected angels: the circle of the "Aura of the Holy Soul" and its importance to human beings and the seven virtues.

Lucifer, when he learned of the important confession of the archangel, looked at him and said: "You will no longer return to the kingdom of Heaven, now you will be my ally and I will transfigure you in a strange way, as if you had never been the creation of Yahweh".

Archangel Egerius fearing Lucifer's promise to turn him into something insignificant, fell to his knees on his feet and said: "Let me return to Heaven and there, infiltrated among your enemies, I will obtain confidential information and report it to you ". Lucifer let out a laugh and a fiery flame for the wind and, without paying attention to the proposal of the archangel Egerius, turned him into a horrible monster to scare even the devils of his underworld. Archangel Egerius could no longer fly and speak, only think and suffer the pain caused by him.

Lucifer, upon learning about the seven virtues of Yahweh to be bestowed on humans, met urgently with Beelzebub and Satan, in order to elaborate, also, seven items totally opposed to the Creator's virtues. Beelzebub advised him to make each item elaborate in the light of seduction, which would cause humans admiration, attraction and enchantment. In this way, Lucifer would cunningly persuade all of humanity, inclining it to error.

Yahweh received news and reports on everything that happened in Heaven through Sabah. This made Yahweh know that everything in heaven, among all hierarchies, was in perfect order. Yahweh, by means of Sabah's accounts, remained calm on his throne at the service of new projects to be applied in Heaven and the Universe, including, especially, Earth. He was studying ways to destroy the "terrible lizards" and also to prevent Lucifer from having free access to Earth, preventing him from polluting it. Yahweh, therefore, would have to remain calm, because, He would have to fulfill the promise to only return to the Universe and visit Earth, when the prototype couple of human creation reached its seventh generation. When that happened - and it was very close! - He would travel through the Universe and visit Earth to obtain the result of the perpetuation of each of its living species, and, finally, to verify the power of Nature's action over everything and everyone.

While Yahweh waited for the moment to return to the Universe to visit Earth and evaluate all of his creations, Lucifer, in his underworld, lectured with Beelzebub, Satan and some leaders - what he called demons or devils - to create strategies in order to convert men on earth against all the principles of Yahweh. He, as the main lecturer, said: "We will integrate with the Earth and infiltrate among humans, teaching them to explore it in all their senses, the values of seduction. We will keep them trapped in the large communities they call villages and, disguised as humans, we will teach them to take care of relevant tasks, the degree of importance of which will insert acts of justice through a set of rules that emanate from power arbitrary to that of Yahweh. These acts of justice will be reversed from that of the Creator".

Lucifer continued his speech by explaining to everyone each of the laws or norms designed and written by him and his dome. These laws would be summarized in seven: the first, gluttony, making them want to have things more and more, without ever being content with what they had; the second, covetousness, making them excessively attached to wealth, making them put aside everything that was sacred and related to Yahweh; the third, lust, making them awaken to the passionate and selfish desire for bodily and material pleasure. This pleasure, suggested by Beelzebub, would, therefore, cause humanity to become attached to carnal pleasures, which, obviously, would generate corruption of customs, extreme sexuality and lust. The fourth, anger, leading them to an intense and uncontrolled feeling of anger, hatred, resentment that may or may not generate feelings of revenge. It would be a mental feeling capable of generating conflicts for the agent that causes anger and anger; the fifth, envy, making them desirous of possessions, status, skills and everything that others have and achieve. The envious would become able to ignore all that is and has to covet what is next; the sixth, pride, making them manifest pride and arrogance. Pride would be their excessive admiration and arrogance, the pretext of becoming superior or better than others, showing attitudes of contempt for others; and finally, the seventh, laziness, making some humans averse to work, often associated with leisure or vagrancy. This last item, according to Lucifer, could have a series of drastic consequences for the next. Lucifer found all these acts of injustice, against the Creator, very, very well!

Later, Lucifer prepared the devils by transfiguring them into humans. He called them demos - "devils in disguise in humans who would act among men with the harmful wit". When transporting them to Earth, he said: "You will infiltrate this vast world and inhabit the most advanced regions of it. Here, you will keep men engaged in various forms of work, leading them to greed, whose behavior will cause them to inadvertently act wrongly against the principles of Yahweh. Know, therefore, that the primary cause of all the principles of Yahweh, on Earth, was proclaimed by the seven angels that, wrongly, I humanized them under the performance of the transformation of appearance and not of conscience..."

Lucifer, before leaving the demos on earth, elected one of them as a leader and, looking for a name that meant "to launch through his demos against the Lord", named that leader the Devil. He instructed the Devil with tasks, handing him a map containing the representation of a part of the Earth where the regions were most inhabited and noting the types of tasks he would teach human beings. Although Lucifer knew that the demos would remain on Earth for long years, he, thinking of Yahweh's promise to visit her, after the twenty-first generation of the prototype couple, decided to apply the extra-sensory communication technique to the demos and, after teaching them this technique, he called the leader of the demons in particular and said: "When you notice a different signal coming from space, be it day or night, collect it in your home and, through an extra-sensory thought, communicate the phenomenon to all and bring them together to return together to our world.

Yahweh has a promise to come back here and, as we don't

know when, it is better to stay alert. I don't want him to discover us in disguise among humans..."

Lucifer, before leaving the Earth, observed some families quietly harvesting the wheat and said, maliciously, by soliloquy: "How much wealth spread through these vast fields of the Earth, Yahweh gave humanity the wheat, rich in starch, which the families harvest , grind their grains and make flour, the basic raw material for their main foods. I am going to make it difficult to harvest wheat, as well as other crops, spreading the seed of evil, giving rise to what I will call chaff, proposing more hard work to humans, so that they do not have time to think about Yahweh or to thank him for everyday staple food ". Lucifer rubbed his hands, raised a handful of seeds and blew them between the wheat fields and other crops. Hence, weeds of various species were born among the abundant plantations, making it difficult for humans to cultivate and harvest various messes. In carrying out this last task, he traveled calmly to his underworld.

When demos and their respective leader or devil settled on planet Earth, they observed that humans were only concerned with subsistence agriculture, hunting and fishing and, sometimes, in the search for strategies to defend themselves from the terrible lizards.

The demos disguised as humans, all in the skins of noble and handsome men, arrived as foreigners to tribes and villages and when they infiltrated communities, they ended up becoming leaders due to their innovators.

Due to Lucifer's plans to keep humans occupied, humanity progressively evolved and men arrived at great discoveries, through their constant explorations of the earth. In this investigative mode, men discovered copper and manufactured various sharp objects and more effective instruments for agricultural cultivation, favoring them in cutting down forests and hunting and fishing practices with the use of well-erected spears. Over time, as stated in Lucifer's plans, they also began to use sharp instruments, such as weapons, and learned to loot villages and tribes to unfairly inherit all the goods of others and, at times, to dominate the alien inhabitants and make them his servants, causing damage to the clans and their important ethnicities. This type of evil aimed at greed was growing in some regions of the planet Earth, taking away peace between the villages and tribes that wished to live in peace under the protection of Yahweh.

Lucifer's demos have, through the ages, that men have also discovered other types of metals, such as tin and bronze, teaching them to also process fire and giving rise to new utensils for important uses, such as the sharp sword, enabling men to use them to cause bloody battles with their fellow men.

Men had the need to take things from one place to another and, with the domestication of animals; they invented an effective means of transport, making use of the humps of camels and the loins of horses. Over time they invented the wheel and, after perfecting it, introduced it as a means of transporting things through animal attraction, making it the greatest invention of mankind, assisting in agriculture, the manufacture of ceramics and the extraction of water from the sources of cisterns.

Villages grew and gained new and increasingly complex characteristics. Many tribes, formerly ruled by clan systems, were almost banished from the Earth phase. This was due to the fact that the villages became densely populated areas, giving characteristics to the first cities.

The belief in Yahweh instituted by the seven humanized angels on Earth was diminished, as men came to believe only in what was visible and brought effective results in terms of material comforts. Owning assets was about men being empowered and they thought it was very good.

CHAPTER 12

JAVÉ VISITS THE EARTH

The Village of Node, which was characteristically a large city, due to its completeness, although it was the only village capable of preserving the ancient beliefs rooted in the seven humanized angels, faced the difficulty in maintaining the services of the "Temple of Heaven" and the "Yahweh's alibi" bonfire.

Agriculture and livestock played an extremely relevant role for the survival of all the inhabitants of the land and the village of Node had great potential in the cultivation of wheat, rye, oats and other various types of cereals, in addition to raising sheep. , making these activities gain market value and generate good profits for producers. From time to time this village suffered invasions by men from rude and savage civilizations who plundered their goods, their provisions and, at times, abducted their women and children, making them their servants. Therefore, the men of this village, as well as many others, reinforced lookouts, watching them day and night. Due to this concern to watch over the village of contraventions, the men no longer went up every seven days in the "Temple of Heaven" to contemplate Yahweh. As this no longer happened, they also ceased to practice the sacred "Yahweh's alibi" bonfire ceremony over time. In this way, the belief instituted by the seven humanized angels, about the importance of knowing Yahweh and thanking him for all the creation instituted on Earth, detracts from their religious culture.

The prototype couple, the progenitor of all clans of the tribe, Node and Avena was elderly when they met their twenty-first generation. This generation took place with the birth of a man, the result of the union of one of his twentieth grandchildren. The birth of this child was a cause for celebration in Village of Node and no one was able to explain why the celestial dome shone with such beauty, since the stars were suspended in large amounts in the endless ether.

The Devil, seeing the bright stars in the celestial vault, noticed something strange and, remembering Lucifer's warning, met with some demos close to him and gave orders to collect. All demos spread over various regions of the planet Earth communicated extrasensory and all retired to the leader's house that night. The next day, before the sun rose and without saying goodbye to the humans, they fled to the underworld of Lucifer.

The birth of the twenty-first grandson of Node and Avena served to signal to Yahweh, on his throne, that the time had come for Him to fulfill his promise to enter the Universe and visit Earth to see the result of all creation instituted in it, for him, Yahweh, confident that everything in Heaven was flowing perfectly well, invited the filial angel, Emmanuel, to take care of his throne, saying: "The time has come to fulfill a promise to return to the Universe and, mainly, the Earth. The visit will be long-lasting, because I will make a thorough assessment of everything that it establishes there. However, I entrust to you, Emmanuel, my throne and the power of all the control of Heaven. When I return to my throne, everything will be linked in one and then, from this pinnacle I will reign, with all my omnipotence, before my, face all my creations and creatures".

The angel Emmanuel conferred with Yahweh and obtained the concession from Him to invite him to sit beside him, the angels Gabriel and Rafael. Gabriel would sit on the right and Rafael on the left, because the angel Miguel would continue alone, to superintend the Celestial Army.

For a long time, the archangels Sabah and Dom searched for Egerius among the different hierarchies and, because they did not find him, they thought that this archangel would be plotting some action plan on the sly to riot the heavenly angels against them and be elected to the throne of Yahweh. The idea of insurrection against Yahweh, imposed by Sabah and Dom, filled Heaven with mystery and the angels, who joined their movement, remained silent at their posts awaiting the order to act against the Celestial Army.

Sabah was informed by one of the seraph angels that reports on all hierarchical orders should be given to the angel Emmanuel, making him understand that he would occupy the throne of Yahweh, until further notice. Sabah was told that Yahweh would be absent from Heaven during a timeless visit to the Universe. This news made Sabah hesitant, as he did not know whether he was jealous of Emanuel on the throne, or was happy with the absence of Yahweh. The absence of the Creator would urgently facilitate the realization of the upheaval that he intended to do in Heaven. He isolated himself from all the angels in his hierarchy to shape some plans for quick and definite action.

Archangel Dom did not give up looking for Egerius. He went to the fort and was informed there by one of the angels in the Celestial Army that Egerius was in the underworld of Lucifer. Dom did not want to believe this, but realizing Egerius' delay in returning to the hierarchy, he ended up convincing himself that the angels of the Celestial Army were right. He then decided to seek out Sabah to let him know about his discovery about Egerius. When Dom found Sabah isolated from the archangels of his hierarchy, he informed him of Egerius' possible whereabouts. The two archangels, fearing they would be betrayed by Egerius, reinforced a hypothesis that he had joined Lucifer in exchange for an important hierarchy in Heaven. They were furious and, taking advantage of the information that Yahweh would be absent from Heaven, increased his campaigns wishing to emerge, urgently, the insurrection, which would not only be against the Creator, but also against Lucifer.

The campaign for the uprising against Yahweh and Lucifer was growing secretly among all the heavenly angels who joined the campaign. They collected daggers, which were taken from the Celestial Army by some angels responsible for protecting them. With the daggers hidden and everything almost ready, Sabah and Dom were waiting for the right moment to start the celestial war.

Yahweh gave Emmanuel the throne and made him sit on it; he

possessed the angels Gabriel on the right and Rafael on the left; visited all hierarchies and the Celestial Army advising them of the new orders from Heaven which would be in Emanuel's custody. As he said goodbye to everyone, He traveled through infinity reaching the entire Universe.

When traveling through the Universe, Yahweh observed the galaxies, the stars and the planets and some empty regions in it, which objective would be for it to expand slowly, bringing together all its beings, infinitely. From the Universe, He observed the Earth and saw the fields, the lands, the plains, the plateaus, the rivers, the seas and everything that He had created on it. He, not containing the emotion of returning to Earth, as soon as he contemplated it, descended on it, landing on the same mountain where He blessed everything and everyone in the Universe, when he finished creating the world. When he stepped on the mountain, he again smoked like a furnace that was shaking greatly, and when he stopped smoking, hundreds of sheep came to meet Him and surrounded him. Yahweh observed that below the hill on which He stood there was a small village and some families lived there. These families lived to shepherd the flocks, this being a common activity among them, in the art of shearing them and making fabrics with wool to cover their bodies and supply their basic needs for food. He blessed the sheep and extended his blessings to all the families who cultivated the sheep, saying: "I will be the same thing for the earth as I am for those families who care for their sheep. Humanity will be my sheep and I will become her shepherd, ready to care for my flock, whatever its size".

Yahweh took a little lamb in his arms, passed his hands lovingly and said: You are a tenuous, naive, chaste and pure animal, you know how to die with dignity, you don't complain about circumstances and you never run away or fight the enemy, you live peacefully and get lost wandering aimlessly. If you don't have a pastor to lead you or defend you, you will easily fall into the enemy's clutches". When Yahweh said this and put the little lamb on the ground, some wolves appeared on the mountain wanting to attack the sheep. The sheep were preserved in the same way and Yahweh raised his hands and put the hungry pack to flight, saying: "Behold, I will do this to mankind; those who come to me, like these sheep, will never be forsaken. I will be a shepherd and to my flocks, I will not miss anything". He made a small gesture to mention the sheep, and the sheep, understanding his sign, left the hill in a row towards the small village.

When the sheep procession entered the village, it drew the attention of all the inhabitants, who, it is not known why, received them with a big party.

Yahweh left the hill and visited the fields and enjoyed the pure smell of rosemary flowers and was happy to see bees and other insects sucking their nectars. He associated nectar as a sacred symbol of wisdom, spiritual enlightenment and also of healing and renewing life. Then He came across wheat fields and some other species of cereal and saw in a small village men, women and children harvesting them for food supplies. He remembered the bread of life and its covenant established between the heavenly angels. When walking around other regions, He came across the terrible lizards and remembered the confession of the seven resurrected angels who had passed on Earth, among humans. He observed them with full attention and seeing them out of touch with nature, stopped for a moment and thought about doing something to destroy them, later introducing them to the primitive form of the prototype of his creation. He made the giant lizards gather in a steppe plain, where the vegetation was a little dense and looked at the infinite, closed his eyes and claimed the destruction of these beings. A flaming-tailed comet came from heaven and surrounded it by a flaming tail comet, which, upon falling into the steppe plain, destroyed the enormous lizards, leaving a crater as a result of the strong impact. To the terrible lizards that were found in other regions, Yahweh made them disappear, gradually, affecting them to some types of pests, caused by dipterous insects and problems in their food chains.

When Yahweh visited the sea, He came upon the huge fish of the cetacean specimen that devoured the fish indistinctly, making it difficult for the perpetuation of the various marine species, to the point of extinguishing them. He was concerned about this fact and seeing this divergence obtained by Lucifer, he immediately thought of destroying them, proceeding in the same way as the terrible lizards. But as the comet had done a huge amount of damage in a certain region of the Earth, He gave up, choosing to return the cetaceans to their original forms of their creation: whales, sperm whales, dolphins and porpoises were reduced back to their original sizes, continuing life in the sea in perfect order.

CHAPTER 13

THE DEATH OF NODE AND AVENA

Since when Yahweh became absent from Heaven, the archangels Sabah and Dom had invested themselves safely in the project of war against the heavenly angels. They prepared the angels adhering to their plans to insurrect the use of daggers, distributing them among them and making them train on the sly.

The seven archangels who had adhered to the Sabah and Dom plan conferred and found that the uprising against Yahweh should not happen, because if the Creator was the great Father, endowed with love and mercy, another who would take His place, never it would be. They watched Lucifer, Sabah, Dom and Egerius claim the power to rule over everything and everything, and their desires to become equal to the Creator stemmed from an act of hatred brought on by someone else's success and possessions. Therefore, the seven archangels concluded: "That would not be good" They decided to distance themselves from the Creator's enemies, meditating on the following term: "Accipere quam facere praetat injuriam". (Rather suffer the harm than do it.). When exchanging information and discussing the issue of upheaval against the Creator, they observed that the speeches of the three transgressors were argued on the simple fact that the heavenly angels were slaves to Yahweh. But that was not true, each, according to their hierarchy, performed their work and as their life was perennial, it would be fair for everyone to fulfill their obligations. Thus, as the angels of Heaven served the Creator, He also served them by drawing on his mercy and sublime love. In any case, they concluded, anyone who came to power would influence anything and everyone, and among Yahweh and the rebellious candidates, the first was effectively the Creator and Father of all things. "Timor Domini initium sapientiae est". (The fear of Yahweh is the beginning of wisdom).

The seven archangels also advocated the act of creating and transforming and came to the conclusion that Yahweh had the power of creation, whereas the rest, that of transformation. To create persisted in giving existence from nothing, because to transform would simply be to give new shape to something or things preset. Then, they also conferring that they spoke to the filial angel Emanuel about the alleged upheaval idealized by the four offenders, it would not be an act of treason, but a possible correction of thoughtless acts, capable of causing damage to all creation and creature intuited by Yahweh. They flew to the pinnacle, and when they were received by the filial angel Emanuel, he revered him as Yahweh's beloved son and made him, in confession, aware of all the problems generated by Lucifer, Sabah, Dom and Egerius, about the possible rebellion.

Emanuel heard in confession the accounts of the seven archangels about the possible uprising in the sky planned by Lucifer, Sheba, Dom and Egerius. He was outraged, especially at the three supreme angels Sabah, Dom and Egerius who invited the angels to a war against Yahweh.   Emanuel, after the confession of the seven archangels, ordered the angels Gabriel and Raphael to open the files "De ordinem caeli" (On the orders of Heaven) and to review the latest reports presented by the archangel Sabah. The two angels studied the reports and assured Emanuel that everything in Heaven, in each hierarchy, was in perfect order. Emanuel, however, asked the angel Alf to send, with the chariot of fire, the archangel Sabah, to make him present on the pinnacle, in front of the throne he was occupied with. Alf carried out the order and in a few moments he had brought Sabah to the pinnacle, making him approach Emanuel.

When Sabah arrived before the throne, he avoided bowing or

looking at Emanuel and the two angels who were sitting on his left and right sides. Emanuel observed Sabah's way of doing things and yet he excused it. Sabah, a little hurried, wanting to know what his presence was about in that sacred place, said: "I believe I sent the last reports to the great filial angel of Yahweh, about all the works performed in Heaven, according to the orders of each hierarchy" . Emanuel signaled a "yes" and replied: "I read them and, for the first time, I asked the angels Gabriel and Rafael to go to the files "De ordine caelestium!" (About heavenly order!), to take and review them. They, however, claimed that Heaven was in perfect order. But what makes you come here is not about that, but about an assignment of a secret mission that you were chosen to fulfill it".

When Emanuel said "secret mission", Sabah looked at him, scared and a little confused. She asked him with an anguished tone: "What is the task for me, magnificent Emanuel? I do not know if I am prepared to perform any other function, except that of reporter from Heaven. As you know, I am just a simple angel". Emanuel replied: "Heaven is a state of eternal fullness of the angels with Yahweh and no angel, in any hierarchy, it is insignificant, Sabah. We are all important in the Creator's perpetual fullness. We are what we are and summed up as a result of our Father's will to make us exist..."

Before Emanuel concluded the answer, Sabah defended himself: "This result, based on the Creator's will, also depends on the free will of his creatures. I believe that if we always do His will, we will never have the chance to know how to do our will..." Emanuel reflected quickly and asked Sabah: "And what would the angels' will be under the protection of free will"? Sabah replied seriously, "Are you sitting at the throne of Yahweh on his will or on His will"? Emanuel replied: "About His will, which will be mining forever". Sabah continued: "Then you will live your life, the life of Yahweh"? Emanuel, cautiously, replied: "Yes, why not connect my life to Him, and become Him in one body, in one spirit?! All the elementary principles of knowledge and Being abide in it, and if I make any choice contrary to Him, I know that I will perish. Yahweh gave rise to all beings and the world to provoke Him and everything he created pleasant situations and circumstances, aiming at equal rights and duties".

Sabah deflated the arguments and, interested in knowing about the "secret mission", the one he was being asked to fulfill, asked: "What is the secret mission competed for me"? Emanuel brought him closer to the throne and replied: "Yahweh is absent from the throne and I occupy him not doing my will, but His. I am not sitting on this throne on the glory of power, but on the obedience due to my Creator and that do not imply any status to me, but the responsibility to govern Heaven under the aegis of the laws of Yahweh whose principles emanate from justice. I know that a large number of angels are joining in an uprising campaign against Yahweh, and that act, unfortunately, will be against everyone, because Yahweh will not endure injustice and He, being what he has always been, will never be removed. He is not the power, He is the emanation of the power and no angel can take His place. The power desired by the contravening angels was in the fact of possessing what Yahweh instituted, but if he happens to be destroyed, nothing will survive without him. If he happens to be restored to power, he is the power emanating, capable of all mysteries be understood only by Himself. Therefore, Sabah, you who are the archangel, chosen and entrusted by Him, the reporter from Heaven, I ask you to fulfill the following mission. Be with Yahweh and with all the angels, a loyal and sincere archangel. Use all hierarchies and convince the angels, supporters of the uprising campaign, to repent and gather before this throne to confess their mistakes and get rid of Lucifer's cunning lies. All will be forgiven and become free from the penalties that will make them eternal servants of Lucifer. Do this secretly; talking to each of the angels and make them disarm their daggers, returning them to the Celestial Army, whose corporation was authorized by Yahweh to make use of them. Make them understand that any contravening angel who raises his dagger against the justice of Yahweh will be worthy of punishment; not from punishment imposed by Heaven, but coming from the devices of Lucifer himself".

Sabah felt a little ashamed at Emmanuel's sharpness and, suddenly, kneeled before him, saying: "I will do what you are entrusting to me, for the love of my Lord Yahweh, Creator and my Father" Emanuel answered him insightfully: "Get up if Sabah, every creature owes only Yahweh and not His angels; however, it is up to me only a warning served as advice, there are angels in Heaven asking the Lord Yahweh for passwords to do and others asking for passwords to fall".

Sabah stood still ashamed, and when he returned to his hierarchy, he stopped to think about Emmanuel's order to disarm the chosen angels voluntarily to the uprising against Yahweh and his final advice. Even though he knew that he was one of the angels "who asked for passwords to fall," he thought wickedly: "I will take Emanuel the misdemeanor angels and these, when they show repentance, will make him a pleasant surprise!" In doing so, he would also avenge Emanuel. He thought of devising a plan with the help of the archangel Dom, but he thought it better not to tell him what happened between him and Emanuel.

In the underworld, Lucifer received demos and their respective leaders sent to earth. When he heard about the strange sign of Heaven involving the source of stars, he was very sure that Yahweh had entered Earth. If his hypothesis were right, he would have to act quickly to carry out the uprising against the Creator's faithful angels. He thought of several action plans, but he was cautious. So he wished to survey Heaven in all hierarchies to study the main field of his battle. He, remembering to have the angel Egerius, as a hostage, dominated his mind, transformed him into an archangel again and made him investigate the angels of Yahweh, in the respective hierarchies. Egerius, under the mental interference of Lucifer, returned to his hierarchy in the kingdom of Heaven and there, upon meeting Sabah and Dom, at the height of the preparation of the insurrection, tried to persuade them saying that he was spying on the kingdom of Lucifer to find out the way of how he and the devils would attack the kingdom of Yahweh. He deceptively made them know that Lucifer would not make the rebellion in Heaven, but on Earth, where Yahweh was among the weak humans. Sabah and Dom believed Egerius' accounts and both were concerned, because if Lucifer defeated Yahweh on earth, he would return to Heaven and sit on the Creator's great throne to rule everything and everyone.

The angel Egerius visited all heavenly circles and obtained information that all the angels adhering to the Sabah and Dom campaign were armed with daggers and ready for battle and that the throne of Yahweh was being occupied by the filial angel Emanuel.

After obtaining the necessary information, Egerius sneaked back to Lucifer's underworld and didn't even need to know everything he witnessed during his quick return from Heaven, because Lucifer, using his evil cunning, accompanied him mentally, without needing to leave his throne. Lucifer again deformed the archangel Egerius and ordered the devils to arrest him in one of the dark dungeons, newly created to arrest the angels of Yahweh who were captured in the war. He met with Beelzebub, Satan and some leaders of the devils for the preparation of the uprising against Yahweh and the heavenly angels.

Dom and Sabah, fearing that Lucifer would defeat Yahweh on Earth and return at any moment as the eternal governor of Heaven, with the power, position, authority and glory stolen from the Creator, became concerned and, before that, precipitated the revolt. Sabah, however, had a tricky idea and, without sharing it with his friend Dom, prepared a quick report and sent it to the angel Emmanuel.

At the pinnacle, Emanuel was absolutely sure that Sabah would not fulfill his secret mission and, to prevent himself, he asked the archangel Michael for help, letting him knows about the possible upheaval idealized by Lucifer which could occur at any moment in Heaven, due the absence of Yahweh. Miguel handed a dagger to Gabriel and another to Rafael and said: "You will be well protected, son of Yahweh, as you have two great gladiators on your right and left side, who will know how to use weapons properly. As for the Celestial Army, everything is under control". Emanuel argued: "I am informed that many daggers of the corporation are in the hands of angels from various hierarchies, who have adhered to Lucifer's conspiratorial plot." Miguel was calm and replied: "I know that and we must not fear, because the powerful daggers are under the power of the angels who will not betray us. I prepared them and let the soldier angels, conspirators of the movement, steal them and place them in the hands of the traitorous angels. I therefore anticipate that they will have great surprises!" And he closed the speech saying: "Bellum sine bello", that is, war without war.

Miguel, after reassuring the filial angel Emanuel, left the throne and hurriedly withdrew from the pinnacle to return to the fort and defend Heaven under any threat from Lucifer or any of his competitors.

When Miguel left the pinnacle, one of the messenger angels went to Emmanuel's throne, made the necessary references and handed him a sign from Sabah, the reporter. Emanuel checked the sign and there were reports affirming it about peace and tranquility in all the hierarchies of Heaven. Sabah made Emanuel believe that there was no angel, from any of the celestial circles, capable of adhering to the Lucifer rebellion. In the end, he revealed about Lucifer's plan to leave for Earth, with his "angels", to rise up against Yahweh and humanity.

Emanuel, when reading the report established by Sabah, was concerned about Lucifer's attitude in attacking the Lord Yahweh on Earth and was forced to do something urgent. He left the throne in the care of the angels Gabriel and Rafael and moved to the Celestial Army to exchange ideas with the angel Miguel on the possibility or not of Lucifer to pass beyond Heaven and be on Earth where Yahweh was visiting his creatures. Miguel denoted that "yes", because to the evil spirit, unfortunately, "everything could".

Emanuel told Miguel about Sabah's report listing Lucifer, with his "angels", in revolt against Yahweh and all mankind on Earth and asked him for action plans to help Yahweh if there was a Lucifer uprising there. Miguel reassured him, making him understand that Sabah's account was wrong, as he had sent angels from the Celestial Army disguised as angels according to each hierarchy, as spies, to obtain accurate information about the possible act of upheaval. in Heaven and, as it was, everything would be ready to happen. Miguel said: "Lucifer has over his power a betraying archangel from Heaven, called Egerius. He tried to link himself to Lucifer in order to gain advantages and ended up being unsuccessful, becoming a defendant condemned to live sufferable in the skin of a monster. Lucifer made use of Egerius to investigate the entire kingdom and to persuade his friends Sabah and Dom that he and his "angels" or "devils" would attack the Earth in due course. In this way, I realize that Lucifer's cunning is to put into practice a plan capable of marching us to Earth with our Celestial Army and leaving Heaven free so that he can take possession of him and reign over the Lord Yahweh's throne".

Emanuel was absorbed when he heard Miguel's reports, and, even more perplexed, when he learned that Lucifer was inventing plans in a playful way, in order to make Sabah believe him and think that he would be doing the Celestial Army a big favor, stating his plan On the report. Miguel woke him up saying that he had excellent plans to defend Heaven against the upheaval of enemies. He warned Emanuel not to leave the throne and, if possible, not to receive any angel, whatever their hierarchy, even second or third orders from the Celestial Army, because the throne was the reason for greed in Heaven between Lucifer and several angels , who believed to acquire, seated in him, the power over all the things created by Yahweh.

While the Celestial Army, under the command of Miguel, was looking for strategies aimed at attacking and defending Heaven, Yahweh, on Earth, clothed in his spiritual essence, visited humans in their respective regions and observed their generations. Humans were busy in their jobs, making tools, inventing things, raising animals and taking care of subsistence and itinerant agriculture. As for the degree of improvement or evolution, Yahweh noticed differences between human groups; some were more evolved and thought of things from the world to the world collectively, perfecting things and achieving success by accumulating wealth and comfort to their groups or themselves; because other groups remained stable, enduring the primitiveness of the habits of life, as to the ways of acting, talking, thinking and taking care of things and of themselves, maintaining themselves in the existence of a stratified society whose objective was summarized in simply live. In an area of the Earth, densely populated, He found a clan different from all his creation, because they are black skin. When observing the clan, He denoted that it was another device of Lucifer and in respect to that transformation, He reflected on the possibility that the dissimilarity of that race advocates other virtues to humanity on the issue of prejudice, which would be a value given to ethical principles . In this way He preserved the genetics of these people, making them stronger, more firm and patient, able to tolerate any adversity. He blessed the clan and made his land spring up abundantly for the prosperity of each family, capable of creating strong bonds of fidelity and mutual identification between them.

Yahweh, observing the ethnic and cultural differences between humans on various sides of the Earth, realized that he should study ways for angels to mediate in the relationship between humans and Him, regarding the process of spiritual and material evolution. The spiritual life would apply to an incorporeal life, to the essence, under the full participation of understanding and understanding; and as for material life, being expressed only by the appearance of things, it would be closely linked to tangible goods, capable of making humans reflect on their fleeting fleetingness. He thought of the work done by the seven humanized angels on Earth in trying to connect humans to the celestial world, making them understand about the importance of knowing the Creator of everything and everything and, mainly, in making them understand about their existence in the world, teaching them solidarity and mutual respect, coexist in daily life. So Yahweh went to visit the village of Node and get to know its generations and the people who lived there.

Village of Node had seven days of celebration, due to the birth of the child who inaugurated the twenty-first generation of the traditional family. On that seventh day, Node ordered his sons and daughters, sons-in-law and daughters-in-law, up to the twentieth grandchildren and granddaughters, to build the "Yahweh's alibi" bonfire in order to end the birth festivities of the twenty-first grandchild with a ceremony of thanks to the Divine Creator of everyone and everything. Some younger villagers criticized Node's generations when they saw them set up the huge fire in the center of the village, and when they tried to put the fire down, after it was armed, they startled everyone when a centrifugal force hurled them away from her. This fact led the old inhabitants of Village of Node to reflect on the values of sacred things and to recount to their children, relatives and friends, about the story of the seven humanized angels who lived among them, in that village.

At night the "Yahweh's alibi" fire was lit. Node preceded the ceremony, making use of the manner taught by the seven humanized angels, and the whole event was confined to the Spirit of Yahweh, who, although they did not know it, was present among them. Yahweh thought everything was very good and seeing that Node and Avena were old and tired, and that they, together, had fulfilled their mission on Earth, took advantage of that sacred moment and, after the fire ceased, made them sit in their armchairs and fall asleep forever.

The death of the Node and Avena couple, although it caused sadness in the village, also served to foster faith in Yahweh to all kingdoms near and far. Yahweh watched the entire ceremony of the couple's incineration, the ways in which the villagers accepted the death of loved ones, and, after evaluating everything, He realized the importance of studying ways to institute sacred doctrines among humans, having as objective of connecting Heaven and Earth; angels and men. This He would call "religion", meaning "rewire", attributing the actions of binding, uniting and securing with the same sacred bonds men and angels to Him. Yahweh concluded by soliloquy: "Everything that connects on Earth will be connected in Heaven, and everything that is disconnected on Earth will be disconnected in Heaven".

As religion would be reverence for His sacred things, Yahweh sensed caution, because only with the passage of time would humans acquire sufficient reason to understand about Him, who was, eternally, responsible for the creation, ordering and support of the Universe.

CHAPTER 14

LUCIFER SUBLEVATION

Sabah and Dom, convinced that Lucifer would make the uprising against Yahweh on Earth, with his evil legion, decided to act against Heaven to become Lords of the Creator's throne. Sabah invented a plan to send some angels armed with their daggers to Emanuel's throne to deceive him. The revolting angels would tell the angel Emmanuel that they had defiled Yahweh, by indirectly adhering to Lucifer's plan of upheaval and that, repentant; they would have to confess their faults to him. Emanuel was announced about the presence of the revolting angels and when he learned that they needed to confess due to lack of conscience, he innocently asked the angels Gabriel and Rafael to leave him alone on the throne to receive them.

The revolting angels, who numbered approximately fifty, when they approached the angel Emmanuel, knelt and paid obeisance's to him and, rising together, drew their daggers and took Emanuel hostage. Sabah and Dom suddenly appeared and the two of them ran simultaneously towards the throne to sit on it. The two collided and fell close to the throne. In the meantime, the angels Gabriel and Rafael appeared, carrying their sharp and shiny daggers. They, however, invested themselves against the rebellious angels. The daggers of the revolting angels when they collided with the daggers of Gabriel and Rafael lost their luster and withered like a vegetable in dry weather.

Sabah and Dom, lying near the throne, were desperate to see what happened to their accomplices' daggers. Soon Gabriel and Rafael defeated all the revolting angels, arresting them and sending them in the chariots of fire to the Celestial Army. Sabah and Dom, when they witnessed the arrest of their allies, hurriedly fled the pinnacle, flying aimlessly in search of other revolting angels. Gabriel and Rafael left Sabah and Dom to flee to assure Emanuel that they were absolutely sure that the two were really the authors responsible for the debauchery in Heaven about the uprising against Yahweh.

Emanuel, saved from danger, returned to the throne of Yahweh to occupy it, but, shortly after he sat on it to reflect on the recent event, he heard screams of threats and wars in Heaven. Lucifer broke out with his evil army in order to snatch all the inhabitants of the kingdom of Yahweh.

Lucifer, facing the command of his army, with a third of the angels converted to him, managed to break the barriers of the fort formed by the Celestial Army. He and his army invaded the third circle, where the executing angels of Yahweh's orders were. He randomly decided to make this circle a battlefield. The messenger angels, astonished by the invasion of Lucifer's army, sounded the trumpets warning all the angels in Heaven about the unusual presence of Lucifer and his cursed army.

Sabah and Dom, when they heard the sound of the trumpets, realized that something wrong was happening in Heaven. They also met with the angels attached to them and, all together, armed with their daggers, marched towards the third circle.

The third circle, transformed into a battlefield, began the war under the command of Lucifer, who, announcing his hatred, said that he was there to exterminate everyone and become the Lord of Heaven. that his uprising against the good would ultimately be a success. He, together with his army, believed to dominate the angels of the third circle and all others and also the Celestial Army.

Lucifer, facing the command of his army, with a third of the angels converted to him, managed to break the barriers of the fort formed by the Celestial Army. He and his army invaded the third circle, where the executing angels of Yahweh's orders were. He randomly decided to make this circle a battlefield. The messenger angels, amazed by the invasion of Lucifer's army, sounded the trumpets warning all the angels of Heaven about the unusual presence of the messenger angels. After the resounding of the trumpets, everything in Heaven became silent. Sabah, Dom and the angels attached to them flew quickly to the third circle to become a battlefield in it, too. Upon arriving there, they, without any rules of strategy, when they saw Lucifer's army with the angels armed with daggers, thought they were the angels of their own hierarchy and, foolishly, showed signs of attack. They drew their daggers and parted against the angels, but as they belonged to Lucifer's army, they were soon defeated. Lucifer, thinking that Sabah, Dom and the angels adhering to them were part of the defense tactics of the Celestial Army, barbarously exterminated them. When Sabah, Dom and their angels were killed, Lucifer looked at their weapons and saw them to be broad-bladed, short, double-edged and pointed blades, larger than the daggers handled by his army, plundered them from the dead. and distributed them to his angels.

Lucifer thought he had defeated a part of the Celestial Army and, from then on, the battle made it easier. He, after taking possession of the daggers of the defeated opponents, ordered his army to search the entire circle and, finally, denoting that there was no angel present in that hierarchy, he, wanting to be sure of victory, summoned his army to attack the second circle and then the first. If, by chance, he won the battle in these last two circles, he would reach the pinnacle and seize the throne of Yahweh, becoming the Lord of everything and everyone in Heaven.

The Celestial Army, knowing that Lucifer's evil army was to leave for the second circle, there secretly prepared a strategic environment for attack and defense. The Celestial Army armed with golden daggers whose powers they had to disarm enemies without injuring or killing them, took action, surprising Lucifer and his army. The golden daggers had the power to destroy the daggers possessed by Lucifer, which lost their luster and withered like a vegetable in dry weather. Lucifer became impotent in the face of the power of the Celestial Army when he saw what happened to the daggers just taken from the defeated angels in the first circle.

Faced with possible defeat, the entire army of Lucifer fled into their underworld, as Lucifer, in trying to do the same, had an unexpected surprise. When he tried to escape, he came across the two angels Gabriel and Rafael, who, as they drew their daggers, chased him. The two heavenly angels fought Lucifer and arrested him, making him a defendant to be judged by Yahweh.

Beelzebub and Satan, who had stayed in the underworld, when they saw Lucifer's army flying over there, all frightened by the defeat, as they observed Lucifer's absence, thought that he would be annihilated by the Celestial Army. The two, however, fought among themselves for the throne of Lucifer. This created confusion, resulting in the division of Lucifer's army in two; one to support Beelzebub and one to support Satan. As the two armies had the same strategies of attack and defense through the forces, neither was able to defeat the other. Beelzebub and Satan ceased their battles and decided to divide Lucifer's underworld into two kingdoms, each of which would resign his own, in the face of his ideas.

CHAPTER 15

THE LUCIFER JUDGMENT

Yahweh visited the whole earth and was sad to see that most men were contradictory to the seven divine instructions, violating all its precepts. They, the superior living beings on Earth, were concerned only with accumulating ostensible wealth to the point of harming each other. Through this purely material behavior, men made excessive mistakes in meeting gluttony, greed, lust, anger, envy, pride and laziness. Then Yahweh thought carefully about the behavior of men and, when he was almost determined to destroy them, reducing them to dust, from where they had emerged, He withdrew from a huge wheat plantation and watched it gently. He noticed among this plantation the presence of the infested tares among the crops. He had not shown that bad seed on Earth, which harmed and depreciated the good seeds. While visiting other wheat fields, he saw some men harvesting the wheat with some difficulty. He then reflected, "The good seed was corrupted by mixing with the bad seed. When the good things mix with the bad things they become impaired. I see that the wheat is suffocated by the chaff and the men who cultivate the good seed, to reap good fruits, will be the arduous task of separating the good from the bad. If Lucifer did this evil and others, for men to take care of this arduous task, without giving importance to time for me, he nevertheless left a beautiful lesson to men on how to separate well from evil". Yahweh preserved the chaff in the wheat fields and saw that the mixture of good and evil would serve as a lesson for men. So He decided to return to Heaven and investigate what had gone wrong against humanity and, depending on this discovery, He would judge whether he would give up men on the face of the Earth or not.

Yahweh returned to Heaven and upon sitting on his throne he

was notified by Emanuel of Lucifer's attempt at uprising against Him and all that He had instituted in Heaven. Yahweh, with Michael, visited the third circle and saw there, hundreds of dead angels, huddled together. Miguel related the following to Him: "These angels were unfit for combat; they joined a revolt invented by Sabah, Dom and Egerius. These three archangels also wanted power and did not adhere to Lucifer; they just waited, in due course, for the moment to act, as soon as Lucifer and his army went into action. We learned that Egerius tried to reach an agreement with Lucifer in favor of the insurrection against Heaven, telling him about the possible participation of the angels Sabah and Dom. Lucifer, not trusting him, took the prisoner. Angerius, in an attempt to get away from the situation, confessed to Lucifer about what he knew about the seven resurrected angels, about the circle of the "Sacred Soul Aura", the importance of creating this circle to humans and also about the seven virtues. Lucifer became interested in the information and, despite transfiguring Egerius, kept him as a prisoner in his underworld". Miguel breathed calmly and continued: "Everything indicates, according to our investigations, that Lucifer was on Earth with his devils transfigured into humans. He managed to distort humanity by making contrary use of the rules of the seven virtues".

Miguel took another short break. Yahweh went on in silence, awaiting the outcome of his reports. Miguel continued: "When Lucifer invaded the third circle, Sabah, Dom and the angels adhering to him took advantage of the situation to also rise up against Heaven. But Lucifer, thinking they were a large part of the Celestial Army, used his strategies to annihilate them. Lucifer shouted victory and left for the second circle, where our Army was present to disarm his army. We didn't want to hurt anyone and we used the golden daggers, which made their daggers lose their luster and wither like a vegetable in dry weather. His army ran away, because he became our prisoner of war".

Yahweh listened carefully to Miguel's inquiry and then concluded: "Death is the definitive cessation of life or of the existence of anything that I will create. I never intended to use death in divergence from life, for me everything would be perennial, but unfortunately, I see that my creatures provide unfavorable conditions, making life just a wisp. I will not awaken these angels and make them memorable in the history of Heaven, until I open an inquisition for a thorough investigation of the facts".

Later, being on his throne, Yahweh called Miguel, Rafael and Gabriel to a meeting at the pinnacle. During the meeting, the summit informed him in detail about the bad procedures of Lucifer and of some angels from Heaven who joined him. When the summit assured Yahweh that Lucifer was under arrest, under the surveillance of the Celestial Army, He, although he could destroy or punish him directly, due to the crimes of crime, therefore decided to set up a court to investigate the facts and judge the main defendant in the rebellion.

When setting up the court, Yahweh summoned seven immaculate angels for jurors; the seven resurrected angels and seven more angels from the second and third circles for witnesses. Miguel served him as a defender of the cause in favor of justice and the angel Gabriel, as clerk, in charge of recording the facts that occurred during the jury. It was up to Yahweh to judge and resolve the impasses, since He would be the judge. For the jury, in the court, Yahweh slept all the angels in heaven, leaving only those who would participate in the court to wake up.

The court set up for the trial took place at the pinnacle, where Yahweh specially prepared it so that everything could take place in full condition. Two angels of the heavenly guard entered the court bringing Lucifer. The defendant was placed before the court granted by Yahweh to be questioned about his fault imputations under heavenly laws. Yahweh started the jury, saying to the seven immaculate, sworn angels: "In the name of the heavenly law, I invite you to examine this cause impartially and to pronounce your decision according to your conscience and the dictates of justice". The seven immaculate angels, sworn in, replied: "So I promise."

Miguel got to his feet and began the preaching: "We are here, in this court to judge the defendant, Lucifer, for moral issues of a spiritual and material nature. The same, like all of us, son of Yahweh, raised over all the greatness of the Father, had the audacity to resist the heavenly laws, which are as sacred as Yahweh, urging all of us to join in his projects to make us free, convincingly claiming to be all of us slaves. He argued to the angels of all three hierarchies that Yahweh was demeaning the power of us all, becoming only Him, the omnipotent. Who else in this kingdom would be able to have control over everything and everyone but Yahweh, the Creator and Father of all creatures? Therefore, the adherence of the angels to Lucifer directly implied an uprising against Yahweh and the whole kingdom of Heaven. The first result of the defendant's uprising was to encourage a third of the angels of the first and second hierarchies to adhere to him, persuading them with absurd promises that will never have the power or the conditions to fulfill them. The second result of the defendant's uprising was when he invaded the third level of Heaven, where the battle of his army took place against the combatants of the third corporation of the Celestial Army. This combat was terrible and, due to the power of the transformation of Lucifer, he transformed the angels adhered to him into terrible monsters and ended up leaving unharmed, taking with them, as hostages, seven angels, four of the messengers and three of the executioners of the order of Yahweh. And as if that were not enough, the defendant took the seven hostage angels to the Universe and made them witness horrible things that he outraged against the creation of Yahweh, transforming reptiles and aquatic species into terrible monsters, in order to devastate the Earth. And there, he abandoned the seven angels, making them human, as if that were a great insult to our eternal Father. Everything the defendant did to exterminate and contaminate the Earth, infiltrating, there, the angels or devils adhering to him, to teach humans the various arts, making these weapons conducive to diverting their attention from Yahweh, making them believe about the importance of gluttony, greed, lust, anger, envy, pride and laziness. Finally, the defendant, who seemed to purposely help the angels of heaven, against any type of slavery, denounced wanting power and eternal glory, aiming to sit on the Lord Yahweh's throne and command everything and everyone, according to his will. And what will the defendant do? Obviously it would be the one with a bad reputation, because his underworld in the north of Heaven is characterized by a horrible feeling of disgust, confronting the seraph, the sign of perfection, full of wisdom and beauty given to him, by Yahweh. In this way, taking advantage of the absence of Yahweh, on the throne, he rebelled against Heaven with his army and, due to the patience to use all the strategies of attack and defense, the Celestial Army managed to avoid the violent combat. Therefore, the defendant is present here, called by the name of Lucifer, to be judged on willful crimes against the creation of Yahweh".

After the angel Michael addressed his imputation speech on the crimes committed by Lucifer, Yahweh brought each of the seven angels into court for them to provide clues about Lucifer's actions on Earth. The seven angels, individually, testified about Lucifer's actions on Earth, from the moment they were captured in Heaven and transported there, transformed into humans, punished for greed and, finally, being thrown into the fire of "Yahweh's alibi" . Then the seven angels of the second and third hierarchies entered the court to testify about the Lucifer uprising. As they had witnessed various acts of Lucifer and other angels in heaven, such as Sabah, Dom and Egerius, concerning the insurrection, they became their authentic and valuable testimonies to the wanton.

Yahweh, after dismissing the last witness, made them fall asleep and allowed Miguel to ask questions of the defendant, asking him what was on the file. Miguel asked him: "Lucifer, are you aware that you were a perfect being in all virtues, according to the sacred proposals of his Creator"?

Lucifer gave Miguel a serious look and simply replied: "Yes! And I am also vainly aware that I was nothing more than a simple servant to my Creator". Miguel continued the investigation, saying: "The Creator made him like all of His creatures, although He gave you something more, making you his seraph, His sign of perfection, full of wisdom and beauty, but, like all the angels in Heaven know, you, Lucifer, refused to participate in the Father's plans, showing yourself proud, arrogant and boastful. Yahweh had the just intention of making him your beloved son, to whom He could place all your trust and admiration, but you, unfortunately, were inclined to weakness and cowardice acting in nonconformity with our norms. All of this was due to the ambition of power, wasn't it?"

Lucifer replied, "Just as the Creator has powers, He should attribute it to all of us equally..."

Miguel asked him: "So confess your greed about the power of Yahweh, Lucifer"? Lucifer said "yes", nodding. Miguel continued: "Isn't the powers our Creator has in the way you think you are, Lucifer? It cannot be attributed to itself, but extended to everyone. Power does not apply to authority, in wanting to do with it what it can do as it pleases, but it must have reason or reason to extend it to others, helping it in whatever way possible. If each one thinks of his neighbor with the same feeling of devotion attributed to us, by Yahweh, we will observe, therefore, to possess him. We learned from our Father, that power is in competence to do good things, making them perfect and lasting".

Lucifer looked at Miguel and had a violent incitement, speaking like a dangerous beast: "Yahweh gave power to Emanuel, making him his image and likeness and different from all angels, for not having wings, with the power of translate it all over Heaven, just like Him. He presented it, too, as to his beloved son".

Miguel immediately refuted it: "So it was all jealousy, but before the Father instituted his son, Emmanuel, you already harbored in your feelings the grudge, the envy and the lack of discernment between good and evil. You misrepresented all the virtues of Heaven by inventing the insurrection against us all for the sake of a power to be emanated from it". Lucifer said nothing.

144

Miguel made further inquiries to him, but he also did not get any answers.

Yahweh, satisfied with Miguel's questions and questions, stopped the defendant from asking questions and summoned the jurors to another room in the pinnacle to decide whether the defendant would be guilty or acquitted. Yahweh and the seven immaculate angels, sworn in, returned to the court to present the verdict. Yahweh read the sentence in which he condemned Lucifer as an aggravating crime, with the penalty of being displaced and expelled from Heaven forever, with his phalanx of angels. Lucifer was picked up by the Celestial Army, awaiting orders from the Creator.

To the Creator, known today as God, the name attributed to Him by Emanuel, from then on, it always consisted of creating new strategies to make humanity believe in the authenticity of his creation, in his sublime love; in his compassion, and, above all, in Him, as an infinite and existing entity by himself; the necessary cause and end of everything that exists between Heaven and Earth.

Yahweh silenced, displaced Lucifer and made the only strong and shining light to appear over all of Heaven, making it reveal all good. All the angels of Heaven, who were still asleep in their given spheres, woke up in awe with the new light. Lucifer was blinded by the light and under Yahweh's orders; the Heavenly Army took him to his phalanx of angels. Lucifer's underworld, as it had been divided in two, that of Satan and Beelzebub, in these two underworlds, all, due to the light emitted by the unique light of Heaven, were blind, lost and without direction. The angels of the Celestial Army, under the aegis of the three archangels Miguel, Rafael and Gabriel, destroyed the two underworlds, captured all their inhabitants, defeated them and hurled them, with Lucifer, in a turkey deep, making them park, hidden, underground. In this sphere inferior to Heaven and to the entire Universe created by Yahweh, Lucifer and all his phalanx of evil angels began to see and establish themselves. As time went by, under the powers of transformation, Lucifer designed his new underworld affixed to a radiated sphere of fire, which he claimed to represent all evil. That underground place where Lucifer and his evil phalanx lived changed to hell; the smallest kingdom, among all that exists in the Universe. From his new home, Lucifer supremely invented other upheavals against humanity, rendering him unfit for the privileges of the Yahweh's concessions.

Yahweh simply replied: "The power of transformation was given to the angels in heaven; to the men of the Earth and even to the Universe as a gift to expand". Lucifer, although resentful of the conflicting suffering of wickedness to which he extended himself, replied to Yahweh: "Do what you have to do and know that the transformation will be my power forever!"

After resolving the impasse on the destruction or not of humanity, Yahweh ordered the Heavenly Army to transport the condemned man to the center of the pinnacle to make him comply with the condemnation. Although Yahweh felt foreboding about Lucifer's evil actions, from then on, He would have to respect his free will. He obviously could not destroy the existence of Lucifer and, like the Celestial Army, although he could and did not, it remained for Him to enforce Lucifer's expulsion sentence, with all his phalanx of angels, from the north of Heaven, where they temporarily occupied it. It is up to Him to respect the law in all cases, even though this is extremely strict. Yahweh looked at Lucifer steadily and said: "Dura Lex, sed Lex!" (The law is tough, but it is the law!). There was a moment of silence and then he continued in an almost anguished tone: "I have to enforce the jury's decision".

Before Yahweh summoned Lucifer to the full completion of the sentence, He visited the first circle again and when he saw the bodies of the angels deceased due to Lucifer's uprising again, He blew hard and transformed them into a powdery mist, making them disappear forever. In fulfilling this, He returned to the throne and thought piously of the humanity created by Him, on Earth. In his reflection, He dismissed the idea of destroying it, as he had not yet given her the chance to know the virtues advocated by the seven resurrected angels. Lucifer had seized them and taught them humanity in a twisted way. I thought: "The mistake is due to the hit!" He was vainly aware that His eternal task would be to preserve his creation, whether through eternal bonds or through the bonds of perpetuation, being by generation, the condition given to everything that was instituted by Him, on Earth.

When Yahweh established the project "mutatis mutandis" in Heaven, aiming at the extinction of the three levels and the creation of variable dimensions, summarizing in a large circle, with the sacred pinnacle in the center and around the three hierarchies of the nine Choirs or Angelic Orders, His next step would be to create a single strong and shining light to manifest over all of Heaven, making it reveal all good and, as He feared Lucifer would not tolerate it, He postponed it. Consequently to the jury and to obtain the sentence sentenced to Lucifer and his adherents, He decided, by fulfilling Lucifer's sentence, to create light and make it perennial in Heaven, unlike the Sun, main and central star of the planetary system, without any movement capable of dividing day and night. Heaven would continue to contradict time.

CHAPTER 16

THE NEW LUCIFER' UNDERWORLD

When Yahweh established the project "mutatis mutandis" in Heaven, aiming at the extinction of the three levels and the creation of variable dimensions, summarizing in a large circle, with the sacred pinnacle in the center and around the three hierarchies of the nine Choirs or Angelic Orders, the next step would be to create a single strong and shining light to manifest over all of Heaven, making it reveal all good and, as He feared Lucifer would not tolerate it, He postponed it. Consequently to the jury and to obtain the sentence sentenced to Lucifer and his adherents, He decided, by fulfilling Lucifer's sentence, to create light and make it perennial in Heaven, unlike the Sun, without any movement capable of dividing the day. and night, as He had established in the Universe. Heaven, obviously, would continue to contradict time.

Before Yahweh summoned Lucifer to the full completion of the sentence, He visited the first circle again, and in reviewing the bodies of the deceased angels due to Lucifer's uprising, He blew hard and transformed them into a powdery mist, making them disappear forever. In fulfilling this, He returned to the throne and thought piously of the humanity created by Him, on Earth. In reflecting on humanity, He dismissed the idea of destroying it, as he had not yet given it the chance to know the virtues advocated by the seven resurrected angels. Lucifer had seized them and taught them humanity in a twisted way. I thought: "The mistake is due to the hit!" He was vainly aware that His eternal task would be to preserve his creation, whether through eternal bonds or through the bonds of perpetuation, being by generation, the condition given to everything that was instituted by Him, on Earth.

After resolving the impasse on the destruction or not of

humanity, Yahweh ordered the Heavenly Army to transport the condemned man to the center of the pinnacle to make him comply with the condemnation. Although Yahweh felt foreboding about Lucifer's evil actions, from then on, He would have to respect his free will. He obviously could not destroy the existence of Lucifer and, like the Celestial Army, although he could destroy it and did not, it remained for Him to enforce Lucifer's expulsion sentence, with all his phalanx of angels, from the north of Heaven, where they provisionally occupied. It is up to Him to respect the law in all cases, even though this is extremely strict. Yahweh looked at Lucifer steadily and said: "Dura Lex, sed Lex!" - The law is tough, but it is the law! There was a moment of silence and then he continued in an almost anguished tone: "I have to enforce the jury's decision".

Lucifer, although resentful of the conflicting suffering of wickedness to which he extended himself, replied to Yahweh: "Do what you have to do and know that the transformation will be my power forever!"

Yahweh simply replied: "The power of transformation was given to the angels in heaven; to the men of the Earth and even to the Universe as a gift to expand".

Yahweh silenced, displaced Lucifer and made the only strong and shining light to appear over all of Heaven, making it reveal all good. All the angels of Heaven, who were still asleep in their given spheres, woke up in awe with the new light. Lucifer was blinded by the light and under Yahweh's orders; the Heavenly Army took him to his phalanx of angels. Lucifer's underworld, as it had been divided in two, that of Satan and Beelzebub, in these two underworlds, all, due to the light emitted by the unique light of Heaven, were blind, lost and without directions. The angels of the Celestial Army, under the aegis of the three archangels Miguel, Rafael and Gabriel, destroyed the two underworlds, captured all their inhabitants, displaced them and threw them, with Lucifer, in a deep turkey, making them park, hidden, underground. In this sphere inferior to Heaven and to the entire Universe created by Yahweh, Lucifer and all his phalanx of evil angels began to see and establish themselves. As time went by, under the powers of transformation, Lucifer designed his new underworld affixed to a radiated sphere of fire, which he claimed to represent all evil. That underground place where Lucifer and his evil phalanx lived changed to hell; the smallest kingdom, among all that exists in the Universe. From his new home, Lucifer supremely invented other upheavals against humanity, rendering him unfit for the privileges of the Yahweh's concessions.

To the Creator, known today as God, the name attributed to Him by Emanuel, from then on, it always consisted of creating new strategies to make humanity believe in the authenticity of his creation, in his sublime love; in his compassion, and, above all, in Him, as an infinite and existing entity by himself; the necessary cause and end of everything that exists between Heaven and Earth.